Twelve Nights with Viola & Olivia

The New Countess: Book 1

Lady Vanessa S.-G.

Pacífico Press
San Luis Rey, California

TWELVE NIGHTS WITH VIOLA & OLIVIA
Copyright © 2023 by Hannah Miyamoto.

All rights reserved. No parts of this book may be reproduced without the written permission of the publisher. For more information, contact info@PacificoPress.com, Pacífico Press, P.O. Box 596, San Luis Rey, CA 92068

The characters and events portrayed in this book are fictitious. Any similarity to real persons, living or dead, is coincidental and not intended by the author.

No part of this book may be reproduced, or stored in a retrieval system, or transmitted in any form or by any means, electronic, mechanical, photocopying, recording, or otherwise, without express written permission of the publisher.

First Edition, April 2023.
ISBN: 9798391015260

Editing and Cover design by: Hannah Miyamoto.

Cover image: "Olivia Unveiling" by William Powell Frith (1874). Folger Shakespeare Library Digital Image Collection, Washington, D.C.

Used under a Creative Commons Attribution-ShareAlike 4.0 International license.

Pacífico Press: P.O. Box 596, San Luis Rey, CA 92068

Subscribe to the Pacífico Press newsletter from our website: https://PacificoPress.com

To Dr. E. Leo Victor, with incompensable gratitude.

You deserved more from me, and everyone else.

The New Countess
A Story of Sexy 16th Century Sapphists of Shakespeare

Book 1
Twelve Nights with Viola & Olivia

By Lady Vanessa S.-G.

Edited by Hannah Miyamoto

Pacífico Press
San Luis Rey, California

Table of Contents

Editor's Notes	i
Reader's Guide	ix
Chapter One: "What Country, Friends is This?"	1
Chapter Two "Thy Constellation is Right Apt"	19
Chapter Three "If ever Thou shall Love, Remember Me"	35
Chapter Four "I would Thou were as I would have Thee be!"	45
Chapter Five "Make Tempests Kind, and Salt Waves Love!"	57
Chapter Six "Long Live the Countess!"	73

Editor's Notes

One advantage of living in southern California is frequently meeting fascinating people with diverse backgrounds, including people from foreign countries. In the case of this book, that country is the United Kingdom.

This novel came to us from the hands of an Englishwoman with a title of nobility and an international performing career. She received it from an elder, who discovered it among papers left by the author. She gave it to us with the understanding that the author and she would be strictly anonymous, and that we would publish it for the world to appreciate.

Most of the manuscripts, including the one that is this book, appear to have been written before 1939. However, at least one of her stories references events discovered later. The author may have also written some parts earlier and rewritten them later into the typewritten manuscripts we have today.

Among the terms to which we agreed to for permission to publish this series are that the author must be anonymous. To accommodate the cataloging requirements of libraries and bookstores, we mutually agreed to the pseudonym of "Lady Vanessa S.-G." Be assured that the true name of her ladyship bears no relation to the name we have concocted.

In reviewing the manuscript for these books, several things became immediately apparent. The most important is that the author wrote her novels with the intention that they would never be published, especially not within her lifetime. In fact, she left abundant notes on and with her manuscripts to make her intentions clear.

To write without seeking a large readership may seem incredible and even pointless. However, her decision gave Lady Vanessa the freedom to write what she wanted, without regard to the laws then in force in the United Kingdom, the United States, and other English-speaking countries against publishing works deemed "obscene."

Lady Vanessa's *New Countess* manuscripts, had any publisher wanted to publish one, would have been immediately declared obscene in the United Kingdom, the Commonwealth, or the United States, as long as she insisted on showing same-sex relationships in a positive way. Although lesbianism was ostensibly legal in Britain in her time, the British courts had declared *The Well of Loneliness* by Radclyffe Hall to be obscene, merely because Hall's 1928 book defended homosexuality rather than condemn it.

Although Lady Vanessa may have shared her writing with her friends and family members she trusted, that network must have been small, for a large group cannot keep such secrets too long. Likewise, although she was not a member of the famous Bloomsbury Group, she probably had the novels of modern women writers like Virginia Woolf on her shelves.

One book Lady Vanessa definitely had, as she references it in the margins of her manuscripts and attached notes, is *The First Night of Twelfth Night* by Leslie Hotson, published in 1954. Dr. John Leslie Hotson was born in Ontario in 1897, was educated in Harvard, and focused his life on trying to solve mysteries of British literature. His first major work was *The Death of Christopher Marlowe* (1925) in which he purported to identify the killer of Shakespeare's famous contemporary.

In *The First Night of Twelfth Night,* Hotson claimed to have found documents indicating that one of the first performances of *Twelfth Night* was for the court of Elizabeth I on January 6, 1601, the "Twelfth Night" after Christmas in 1600. The character of "Countess Olivia," Dr. Hotson argued, was inspired by the tendency of the subjects of Queen Elizabeth I to shout "O Live!" when she passed by. In addition, the honored guest for the occasion at which Shakespeare's company performed the play was Virginio Orsini (1572-1615), the second Duke of Bracciano, son of Paolo Giordano Orsini and Isabella de'Medici, brother of the Queen of France, and the husband of a niece of Pope Sixtus V. In other words, Duke Orsini was a proper guest of honor for the English monarch, especially on a Christian Feast Day.

Hotson further claimed that *Twelfth Night* was written as a wish-fulfilling tale for Queen Elizabeth, in that Olivia chooses as her husband a young parentless boy that looks like his beautiful sister. He even claimed to have found an entry in the diary of a Spanish ambassador in which he wrote that Elizabeth had idly asked him about the state of a certain older unmarried Spanish princess, before she expressed that she wished she could marry a daughter of the Spanish king, and thereby retain her power as the monarch of England, while forming an alliance with a potential rival kingdom, and thus advance the interests of her country!

Judging by the marginalia and notes in Lady Vanessa's manuscripts, she had finished most of her manuscripts before reading Hotson's book on *Twelfth Night*. Moreover, if Lady Vanessa had discovered *The First Night of Twelfth Night* shortly after it was published in 1954, she might have been in communication with him while he was a fellow at Cambridge between 1954 and 1960.

If Hotson is correct about *Twelfth Night*, then Lady Vanessa's adaptation and extension of *Twelfth Night* is not mere "fan-fiction," but a legitimate attempt to answer lingering mysteries in Shakespeare's play. For example, *Twelfth Night* never explains why two teenagers, just 16 years old, travel unaccompanied across the sea, after their father had died. In her novels, Lady Vanessa presents Sebastiano and Viola as Greeks nobles threatened by the rapacious Ottoman Turks who have slain their father; rather than allow the Turks to abduct and enslave her children, their mother sends them to a relative in Padua. Unfortunately, their ship founders off the coast of Abruzzi (fictionalized from the real region of Abruzzo, although Abruzzi was one of its historical names), 240 miles (400 km) down the coast from the bustling centers of northern Italy.

Twelfth Night also never explains why Olivia—after foreswearing all the rich and powerful men that seek her—falls helplessly into love with Viola, when she is pretending to be a boy named "Cesario." Lady Vanessa— and here is why her novels were unpublishable until now— shows the countess in a passionate love affair with her chambermaid Maria. However, knowing that she cannot marry and must marry a man, Olivia goes mad for Viola—mad enough to fool herself when Viola's twin-brother Sebastiano agrees to marry her—because she is attracted to women much more than men.

Fundamentally, *The New Countess* is Lady Vanessa's attempt to translate Shakespeare's fantasy into the dangerous world of 16th century Italy, when rival nobles vied for power, land, and treasure, using lies, war, treachery, and murder as they willed. Her novels do not insert her personality into Shakespeare's Countess Olivia, but do show the dangers and challenges that a real Olivia would face in the real 16th century.

One of the dangers a real-life Olivia would face, Lady Vanessa hastens to illustrate, is public execution for having "unnatural relations" with another woman. Besides being true, it also dramatically raises the dramatic tension in Shakespeare's story; despite all she does to hide her secret, her Olivia lives in constant fear that her love for Maria will be discovered, with terrifying consequences for both of them.

Lady Vanessa's graphic description of Olivia and Maria's sapphic relationship shows that, at some point of her life, she must have had at least one relationship with a woman. Indeed, one likely reason she wrote her *New Countess* manuscripts was to record those moments of ecstasy, while knowing that she would never live to see her books published with her vivid descriptions of such joyous exhilarating experiences.

Lady Vanessa's defiance against moral and legal strictures against homosexuality helps explain what she wrote, but it does not explain why she wrote so much that she knew could never be published during her lifetime. I believe Lady Vanessa wrote her *New Countess* manuscripts because Contessa Olivia represented, for her, a wish-fulfilling fantasy character. Although the life of the typical pampered British aristocrat seems to promise ultimate bliss, it would likely not give a woman a life as free as the one Shakespeare gave Countess Olivia, who has no parents, siblings, and but one ineffectual uncle. As a rich, powerful and self-ruling countess, she can choose her husband, and no one can force her to marry anyone.

If Lady Vanessa was like most women in her position, her parents pressured her into marriage and effectively dictated who would be her husband. Her husband just as effectively determined how many children she had, and when she had them. She had little money that was exclusively hers. For all the comfort and luxury that she enjoyed, she was expected to be as decorative, harmless, and delicate as a porcelain figurine on a shelf. Even her title rested upon her like a tiara given to her by her aristocratic husband.

Knowing that, you can see why Lady Vanessa used writing to discover whether she had the potential to be more than decorative and harmless. She wrote her novels for the same reason that other people avidly solve crossword puzzles: She wrote to learn if she could write. In the process, she wrote novels that she wanted to read.

In adapting her writing into these novels, I chose to preserve as much of Lady Vanessa's vision as possible. In addition to maintaining her British English spelling, I tried to incorporate as much of what she typed on paper into her narrative as possible.

What she wrote on the margins of her typewritten pages, or wrote on notes clipped to her manuscripts: These are what raised the most troubles. Knowing that they represented Lady Vanessa's private thoughts, I chose to incorporate as much of her notes and asides into her narrative as possible without breaking the flow of her story; these were her thoughts, and she wrote to communicate her thoughts to her readers, in whatever decade or century that occurred. Another editor might have chosen to produce a more stylized text, or place her tangential thoughts into footnotes.

In *The New Countess*, Lady Vanessa writes dialogue like Shakespeare, and descriptions like Woolf, distilling her frustration with the restrictions set against her into eloquent prose, and expressing her fury and anxieties through the passion of her characters. At the least, her work illustrates that there were such women as Lady Vanessa before it was as safe—relatively—to speak as openly about homosexuality, gender equality, and gender diversity as it is today.

Hannah Miyamoto
Oceanside, California

Reader's Guide

Social Rank and Grammar in the time of Shakespeare

European society in the early modern era was strictly stratified and social divisions were conspicuous and rigidly enforced. In Shakespeare's England, merely using "Thou" to the wrong person could be a major insult. A century later, egalitarian-minded Quakers were harshly punished for refusing to address public officials with the more-obsequious "You."

Although they sound almost-comically ancient today, some English dialects still use "Thou," "Thee,", "Thy" and "Thine." For example, the 2004 song "I Predict a Riot" by the Kaiser Chiefs begins in the Yorkshire English dialect:

> Watching the people get lairy[*]
> It's not very pretty, I tell thee.

Probably to help reflect the importance of social rank in the only partly-imaginary 16th century world that she created, Lady Vanessa wrote the dialogue of *The New Countess* series using the vocabulary and grammar of

---

[*] "Get lairy" is British slang for "become aggressive."

Elizabethan England. You, the reader, will gain much from *The New Countess* novels if you understand the social ranking system that she uses in her narrative, and how the grammar she uses indicates the relationships between the characters.

SYSTEMS OF SOCIAL RANK

The adjacent chart illustrates the system of nobility that Lady Vanessa uses in *The New Countess* series. Titles are in English, with the Italian translation in parentheses. The proper form of address is next to the title. "Viscount/Viscountess" is the lowest rank for which any term but "Sir" or "Madam" is appropriate.

For each rank conveying the right to rule a territory, the name of that title is listed. Boxes that are blank indicate that no land rights generally came with the title. Most of these land units will be familiar to you, except for "March," which refers to a territory that borders another sovereign entity. As a result, a "Marquess" is considered more important than a "Count."

I put "God" at the top to emphasize that the entire social structure of Europe was justified by the principle that the power of all rulers came from God and that all rule was by "divine right."

Systems of nobility changed over time; "gentleman" and "gentlewoman," for example, only originated in the 15th century. However, because those titles were established by the time of Shakespeare, they appear in *Twelfth Night*. Shakespeare, of course, was guessing about Italian noble ranks when he wrote his plays. In reality, systems of nobility varied across the various Italian states.

God		
Title and Address		Hereditary Territory
Pope (Papa)	"Your Holiness"	Christendom / The Papal States
Royalty		
Emperor (Imperatore)	"Your Imperial Majesty"	Empire
Empress (Imperatrice)		
King (Re)	"Your Majesty"	Kingdom
Queen (Regina)		
Prince (Principe)	"Your Royal Highness"	Principality
Princess (Principessa)		
Nobility		
Duke (Duca)	"Your Grace"	Duchy
Duchess (Duchessa)		
Marquess (Marchese)	"My Lord"	March
Marchioness (Marchesa)	"My Lady"	
Count (Conte)	"My Lord"	County
Countess (Contessa)	"My Lady"	
Viscount (Visconte)	"My Lord"	none
Viscountess (Viscontessa)	"My Lady"	
Baron (Barone)	"Sir"	Barony
Baroness (Baronessa)	"Madam"	
Gentleman (Nobile)	"Sir"	none
Gentlewoman (Nobildonna)	"Madam"	
Knight (Cavaliere)	"Sir"	none
Dame (Dama)	"Madam"	
Lord (Signore)	"Sir"	Seignory
Lady (Signora)	"Madam"	
Commoners		

Although a gentleman or gentlewoman ruled no one independently, they chose their own clothes (subject to the sumptuary laws in effect), rather than wear the livery of the noble that they served. That fact helps explain why Viola, while serving as gentleman to Count Orsino, is confused with her brother Sebastiano, who is not serving anyone and is not wearing anyone's livery.

Abruzzi, the county in which *The New Countess* series is set, is within what modern scholars call the Kingdom of Naples, although Naples was actually considered one of the two Kingdoms of Sicily at the time. Naples only became part of the Spanish Empire in 1504, after its army captured the Neapolitan throne from the Angevin dynasty of France.

In *Twelfth Night* and this book, the initial social order of the characters is as follows:

> Count Orsino (ruling)
> Countess Olivia
> Viscount Curio
> Gentleman Sebastiano, Gentlewoman Maria, and Gentlewoman Viola
> Sir Tobi, Sir Andreano
> Higher Commoners: Maggiordomo Malvolio and Signore Fabian

Countess Olivia's pale skin, blonde hair and grey eyes indicate that her ancestry is a mix of Norman French and Lombard, and thus different from that of the new Spanish rulers of the kingdom.

Norman rule over "The Sicilies" began in 1130, when the Pope recognized Roger II as king, after he united the island of Sicily with southern Italy, thus forming "The Kingdom of Sicily." In 1302, the King of Sicily gave up his claim to the island of Sicily, which effectively made Charles II, "King of Sicily," the king of a "Kingdom of Sicily" that did not include the island of Sicily.

However, when Roger II founded the Kingdom of Sicily, the land that Lady Vanessa describes as the site of Piscari was still part of the Holy Roman Empire and known as the "Duchy of Spoleto." From 570 to 774, Spoleto was Lombard territory, before the Lombards submitted to the Franks, although the rulers remained Lombards for centuries.

The Lombards were among the Germanic tribes that invaded northern Italy in 568. According to ancient texts, the Lombards originated in or near present-day Denmark; if that is true, they are related to the Anglo-Saxon tribes that settled England.

Incidentally, the same ancient texts about Lombard history also set forth much of what we know today about "Norse Gods" like Odin and Freya. If Olivia's ancestry were largely drawn from Normans and Lombards, she would likely have the looks that Shakespeare describes, including her grey eyes.

Countess Olivia's Norman and Lombard ancestry in a kingdom ruled by Spaniards makes her vulnerable to being deposed or usurped by any ambitious Spanish noble. Consequently, she moves cautiously to protect her power, using a mixture of servility and diplomacy.

FORMS OF ADDRESS AND SOCIAL RANK

In Elizabethan English, two systems of personal pronouns are in operation.

"Thou," "Thee," "Ye," "Thy," "Thine"

"You," "Your," "Yours"

"Ye" is the plural of "Thee" (e.g., in the Christmas carol "O Come all Ye Faithful"), while "Thy" means "Your" and "Thine" is equivalent to "Yours."

Generally, the "Thou" forms are only used by a superior speaking to an inferior. However, "Thou" forms are also used to signal intimacy, sincerity, and passion.

For example, in Act II, Scene I of *Twelfth Night*, although Sebastian and Antonio address each other with "You" forms when they are together, after Sebastian leaves, Antonio demonstrates how much he loves Sebastian by using "Thou" forms in his soliloquy (emphasis added), and also by ending his speech with a rhyming couplet.

> The gentleness of all the gods go with **thee!**
> I have many enemies in Orsino's court,
> Else would I very shortly see **thee** there.
> But come what may, I do adore **thee** so
> That danger shall seem sport, and I will go.

The dual use of "Thou" forms helps, paradoxically, to conceal Orsino's feelings for Viola in Act II, Scene 4, because he uses "Thou" forms constantly while speaking to Viola (disguised as a boy named "Cesario"), whom he outranks. Viola, on the other hand, never assumes enough familiarity with Orsino to use other than "You" forms.

Lastly, "Thou" forms can be used to express contempt and even hatred. For example, Orsino addresses Antonio with "Thou" after his men have captured him and present him to the Count as a prisoner (emphasis added):

> Notable pirate, **thou** saltwater thief,
> What foolish boldness brought **thee** to their mercies
> Whom **thou**, in terms so bloody and so dear,
> Hast made **thine** enemies?

"You" forms are used by inferiors addressing superiors to show respect, and in other circumstances where the parties are not intimate with each other. For example, Antonio responds to Orsino's insults as follows:

> Orsino, noble sir. Be pleased that I shake off these names **you** give me.

Finally, "Sirrah" is a form of address used by a superior to speak to an inferior man or boy, usually to signal anger or contempt at the same time. For example, in *Twelfth Night*, Count Orsino uses "sirrah" to question his "Gentleman Cesario" when he suspects that he has betrayed him by falling in love with Countess Olivia, who he desires above all else:

ORSINO: Husband?
OLIVIA: Ay! Husband! Can he that deny?
ORSINO: Her husband, **sirrah?**
VIOLA: No, my lord, not I.

Olivia uses "Sirrah" twice in *Twelfth Night* to address her people, specifically when she is giving orders to Feste, her fool, and Fabian, at the end of Act V, Scene 1.

How does he, **sirrah?**
Read it you, **sirrah.**

In conclusion, using words likes "Thou," "Thee," "Ye," "Thy," "Thine," and "Sirrah" serves more than to just sound like "old" English: They provide important information about the relationship between the characters, including their relative social rank, and even their emotions toward another person.

By keeping social rank and the relation of rank to forms of address in mind while you read *The New Countess* series, you will gain a deeper understanding of the story that Lady Vanessa wrote.

Twelve Nights with Viola & Olivia

By Lady Vanessa S.-G.

Chapter One

"What Country, Friends, is This?"

Warm fresh breezes blew across the Adriatic shores of Abruzzi as *Contessa* Olivia, draped in back, rode across her estate with her uncle *Cavaliere* Tobi. A practiced rider, Olivia held the reins of her mount confidently, with her black veil drifting behind her.

Olivia's choice of riding costume did not reflect her sartorial preferences; she would much rather wear the colours of roses, daffodils, and irises, shades that best matched her flaxen hair and grey eyes. However, today her garb indicated that she was mourning the passing of her brother *Conte* Leonato, along with her mother, *Contessa* Sophia, and her father, also named *Conte* Leonato. All had been taken from her in the past twelve months.

With the sudden passing of her brother, Olivia took the family title, and the responsibility for maintaining the place and fortune of the family of which she was now its ranking representative. Without wishing it, without recourse, she was The New Countess.

Walking her horse along the edge of the Castellamare estate, Olivia thought that she and Tobi were alone. However, unbeknownst to her, her distant cousin and the local ruler, *Conte* Orsino, was staring at her through his spyglass, as he stood on the balcony on the north side of his family's house.

To him, Olivia was not only irresistibly beautiful, but in addition, marrying her would unite their respective houses for another generation. However, today Olivia's grace and beauty was most on his mind, as he spoke to his aide, *Visconte* Curio, standing next to him.

"My dear Curio: When first my eyes saw Olivia, methought she purged the air of pestilence."

"Her ladyship is passing fair," affirmed Curio.

As Orsino watched her through his glass, Olivia spied an object out of his view.

At that moment, Valentino, Orsino's trusted chamberlain, joined the two men on the balcony. Orsino, anxious to hear Valentino's report, put down his glass.

"What news, sir?"

"My lord, I would not be admitted," began Valentino, still catching his breath. "But know this from her gentlewoman: The Countess shall mourn her brother for seven years hence; not before shall she entertain a union."

Meanwhile, as Orsino turned his eyes from her, Olivia revealed to her uncle the object of her interest: A young tree, with fronds spilling out, standing scarcely a yard above the ground.

Olivia drew her sword from its scabbard, and with a lusty shout, spurred her horse and slashed through the tree as though it were the neck of an enemy.

Olivia wheeled her horse, sheathed her sword, and at a walking pace, reached down to the severed tree top, and raised it triumphantly. Tobi applauded her display of martial virtue.

"What Country, Friends, is This?"

Had she been aware of Baldassare Castiglione, whose book *Il Cortigiano* (The Courtier) would not be published until 1528, Olivia might have been reluctant to ride her horse at a gallop and carry a sword like a warrior, for it was in this influential book that Castiglione condemned noble families that trained their girls to be skilled with spirited horses and deadly blades.

Instead, Olivia modelled herself after *Contessa* Caterina Sforza, a noblewoman and mother who wore armour and led the defence of Ravaldino fortress against the troops of Cesare Borgia during a siege that ended in 1500.

Florentine diplomat Niccolò Machiavelli, one of Olivia's favourite writers, was among those who praised Sforza's courage.

"Such love for a mere brother!" exclaimed Orsino. "How deep will she love when she has a husband!"

Orsino redirected his spyglass at fair Olivia, as the countess and knight slowly walked their horses out of his sight.

* * *

That night, Olivia's chambermaid, *Nobildonna*, or "Gentlewoman" Maria, spoke with her as she undressed her ladyship.

"That's a foolish knight your uncle has brought into the house."

Twelve Nights with Viola & Olivia

"O, Maria!" said Olivia, as she always preferred to avoid conflict. "If he be honest, we shall suffer his company."

"I have heard thy uncle suggest he be thy husband."

"Tobi knows I'll not marry below my station," scoffed Olivia. "And that hair:" referencing the weakest feature of *Cavaliere* Andreano, "like flax on a distaff!"

"Some hussy may yet take him between her legs and spin it off!" joked Maria.

"Ay, and if it does not come off in a piece!" continued Olivia.

The two women giggled as Maria put away Olivia's mourning clothes. Olivia entered her bed, a huge mattress that would easily bear four adults, covered with ample blankets and a duvet stuffed with feathers, a welcome recent innovation. Stout sculpted posts on each corner hoisted a great canopy above her bed.

Maria closed the door and pushed the heavy latch that barred sudden entry from the hallway. As she turned from the door, Maria's breaths became short with expectation, for she never presumed what Olivia would will.

Olivia pretended to read her book while she watched Maria return from the doorway. As much as she loved Maria, Olivia secretly enjoyed her power over Maria. Merely thinking of that power made her feel sinful, but she could not deny the truth of her sin. Of all she ruled, none were closer to her than Maria.

Maria went to her bed and ruffled the bedding and pillows so to appear as though she had slept in it. When she was done, she turned to Olivia.

"What Country, Friends, is This?"

Without a word, Olivia smiled and nodded to Maria. Maria grinned with joy, removed her gown, doused the one lamp in the room still burning, and stood naked in the moonlight before Olivia.

Olivia pulled aside the covers and hastily removed her gown as Maria joined her. Her first contact with Maria's skin sent electricity through Olivia's body.

Maria lay beside Olivia, knowing that her ladyship must touch her first. Olivia climbed on top of Maria, and licked her lips with anticipation. Now both ladies' breaths were short.

Olivia realized that her lips were dry. She reached over for the goblet of watered wine by the bed.

As she drank, she stared at Maria and asked if she was also thirsty. Maria's nod made Olivia think of slaking Maria's thirst by passing the wine through her kiss.

Instead, she motioned and Maria sat up to take Olivia's cup from her porcelain-hued hands.

After drinking from the goblet, Maria silently offered Olivia more wine. Olivia shook her head and Maria set aside the goblet.

Facing Olivia, Maria felt the warm hands of the countess caress her head as Olivia's wine-touched lips pressed against her own. Maria felt as though her head was spinning, so intense was her love for Olivia.

Olivia reached down with her right hand to stroke the hairs near Maria's thighs. Maria shivered and closed her eyes, enjoying the sensations that Olivia gave her.

Maria pulled away and applied her lips and tongue to Olivia's pre-maternal breasts as the countess pushed back her head to enjoy the sensations her gentlewoman gave her.

Twelve Nights with Viola & Olivia

Holding the higher station, Olivia knew she had no obligation to think of Maria's pleasure. However, the countess refused to use her best friend this way.

The two noblewomen had been stroking and kissing for at least a half-hour, when Olivia stroked Maria's shoulders and whispered softly:

"Lean thou against the headboard."

Maria nodded with understanding and smiled with anticipation. She positioned herself and spread her thighs invitingly. Olivia began stroking Maria's labia with her fingers, as she embraced Maria and kissed her lips. Maria pulsed with anticipation, as she had taught Olivia all the countess knew of female pleasure.

Olivia shook her head and blinked her eyes to regain her concentration. As she pushed her fingers inside Maria, she stroked her maid's hair while watching the response of Maria to each additional inch that she inserted her fingers. Olivia smiled, delighted with her ability to give her gentlewoman pleasure.

Olivia took up a warmed towel made of Spanish cotton, as fine as any in Christendom. She placed it under her chambermaid.

"Ready?" said her ladyship.

Maria nodded, already unable to form words.

Olivia first stroked Maria with two fingers, then three, then four, as her gentlewoman became steadily wetter; to Olivia, Maria's vagina was like a mouth that hungered for the countess, demanding more and more from her. Finally, Olivia introduced her entire hand.

"What Country, Friends, is This?"

Olivia slowly pushed in all her fingers and her thumb. Maria gasped. A loud sloppy sound came out as Olivia's right hand displaced air inside her lover.

Pushing her closed hand to the internal limits of Maria, Olivia slowly opened it, feeling Maria's cervix, then slowly closed it again. Maria shook so hard that Olivia's wrist strained.

Olivia kissed Maria again, but this time she gripped the back of Maria's neck, like a predator taking down prey. Now the two were no longer demure noblewomen but hungry animals locked in passion. In their minds, there was only space for one rational thought: They must make no noise revealing to anyone outside the room what they were doing inside it.

Maria slammed back against the headboard hard; the sound of the impact echoed through the room.

Olivia smiled in delight at what she had caused her gentlewoman to do. Then hastily, clumsily, she fumbled with a pillow and placed it behind Maria before her chambermaid regained her senses.

Olivia came back again to Maria's lips and head. She felt the sweat drip along Maria's hair and knew what she had achieved. Every sign of order in her maid's hair was gone; her lips glowed red from overuse. Her eyes were wet from tears as her emotions spilled from her.

Maria's gasps stopped when her cervix pressed hard against Olivia's hand. Instinctively, Olivia pressed against Maria's cervix to maximize the sensations of her gentlewoman. Involuntarily, Maria's pelvic muscles pressed against Olivia's hand, squeezing that part of the countess.

Twelve Nights with Viola & Olivia

As soon as Maria's excitement abated, Olivia eagerly coaxed another, even as fluids dripped along Olivia's wrist. This time, only a few pushes were needed to trigger another in Maria. Again, the countess felt her gentlewoman's muscles clamp against her arm, joining the two of them together until Maria's excitement diminished and her pelvic muscles relaxed.

After the fourth, sixth, twelfth – who could know? – time, Maria was exhausted. She caught her breath and regained awareness of her birth canal. It started to sting. She gasped for air. Instinctively she placed a hand on Olivia's arm, pushing it away.

"Art thou sure?" asked the countess.

Maria nodded weakly. She felt the sweat on her face and shoulders that had cheered Olivia to take her gentlewoman to ever higher levels of passion.

Slowly, carefully, with her eyes staring into Maria's, Olivia pulled out her wrist, then her thumb, and then all her fingers. Maria found the wait excruciating, but she knew that going gently was the best way.

When Olivia was done, she caressed Maria and kissed her again. There was no need for words. As she knelt between Maria's thighs, Olivia suddenly felt her bare breasts brush against Maria's and her mind told her that she and Maria could never be apart.

Regaining awareness, Maria realized that Olivia's hands and wrist were coated with her vaginal secretions.

"My lady, let me wash that off!"

Before Olivia could speak, Maria tried to leave the bed. She nearly fell.

"What Country, Friends, is This?"

"No, no: Stay Maria! I shall get it."

Olivia, with a clearer head, pushed her long slender legs from the bed to the floor. She felt the chill night air and fumbled as she found her nightgown.

Olivia draped the fabric of the gown over her shoulders and walked carefully through the dark room to a basin sitting across her chamber. She poured water from a pitcher and slowly washed Maria's fluids from her hand. Olivia called to her gentlewoman:

"Canst thou do more this night?"

Maria answered, "In a trice, my lady." Already Maria had begun remembering the difference between them. Olivia scowled at hearing "my lady," but Maria could not see her face as it was turned from her. They had grown up together, but to Olivia, Maria was still always bowing and curtsying and rushing to serve her. Did Maria not know that – but for her – Olivia was alone?

Had Olivia lived at another time, she would have known the passage Shakespeare wrote in *Richard II* in which he relates how even a mighty king feels want, tastes grief, and definitely needs friends.

"Give me but a jot, my lady," said Maria.

"Take from the goblet what thou wills," said Olivia. "Thou must have thirst."

Olivia knew that she had to give Maria permission to share anything with her. "That poor girl would die of thirst shouldst I not give her leave," Olivia thought.

"Ay, my lady," answered Maria, as she reached for the goblet. She raised it to honour her countess. "Thanks to thee."

Twelve Nights with Viola & Olivia

In the darkness, Olivia shook her head. Another "my lady." She understood Maria, but oh – oh – how she would raise her station. "That thought hath no profit,: Maria as my wife," thought Olivia.

To become a countess, Maria would have to marry a man; and then, as the wife of a man, they would be parted. But, thought Olivia, is that what she would have of Maria: "A wife? And she, her husband?"

Olivia remembered what her mother had said when she had innocently told her she wanted to marry her best friend in the whole world, Maria:

> "But maids must sure marry;
> and only to men."

"Midsummer madness" muttered Olivia for even wishing she could marry Maria.

Maria heard her, but as she did not detect a command or request, she remained silent.

Maria watched and admired Olivia's careful patient and methodical washing. "How like her," thought Maria. "Prudent and aware of all details." Suddenly Maria wondered if Olivia wanted to return to bed, but the countess did.

With her senses returned, Maria left Olivia's bed, and retired behind a screen set in the corner. Olivia smiled as she heard Maria make water. "So modest when she hath no secret to me," thought Olivia. Once again, Olivia enjoyed her ability to give Maria so much pleasure.

As Olivia dried her hands, she looked up and away, caught her reflection in the looking-glass, and softly giggled. How strange she looked, wholly naked with her long blonde hair dangling from across her shoulders.

"What Country, Friends, is This?"

She looked down to the blond hair between her thighs and remembered that her body was no different from every peasant woman or girl under her rule. Cleaner, sweeter-smelling, often covered in velvet, satin, jewels and even fur, but under all that, the same female body.

Yet she was a countess who received homage from men, women, and children every day. "How can you say to me I am king?" Olivia would have asked.

Olivia dispelled her musings and returned to her bed with a towel for Maria. Maria enjoyed the sight of Olivia's naked form, one clamshell short of looking like Venus at her birth. Olivia handed Maria the towel.

"This is for thee."

Maria accepted it like a costly gift, and shook her head: "Your ladyship shouldst not serve her maid."

Olivia knew her role in this exchange. "It is what I will," she commanded, sans equivocation. Now, Maria could not refuse.

Olivia continued: "I wouldst not have thee take ill from the night air." Olivia sat on the bed with Maria and gently stroked her skin with the towel, enjoying the sensation through her fingertips.

"Art thou disposed, my lady?"

Olivia would rather have slept in Maria's arms, for she had also exerted herself while loving her maid, but she could not let her gentlewoman think she had tired of her company. Olivia also knew she could not ask Maria what she preferred, as this girl would, for her countess, exert herself until her life-spirit departed.

Olivia, nodded softly and positioned herself against the pillow. Maria's wetness had not yet dried, and the pillow

Twelve Nights with Viola & Olivia

felt cold, but the countess pushed that from her mind. She reached forward to Maria and kissed her, tasting the watered wine as she did.

Olivia stopped, and gently pushed Maria away. The countess raised one thin finger to halt Maria, then leaned over to take the goblet. Maria nodded with understanding.

Olivia drank from the goblet. Maria waited and watched her drink.

Silently, Olivia offered the goblet. Maria accepted a sip. After offering Olivia some more, and being refused, Maria returned the goblet to the stand next to the bed. There was now just a gulp left in the goblet.

Maria knew that only one goblet of wine remained; hers, by her bed. Yet she could not offer her wine to Olivia; the countess must command her to yield it. How she preferred to get her lady a fresh goblet from the floor below, but Olivia always enjoined her. Olivia thought a similar thought, wishing they could simply share wine as friends of equal social rank.

Olivia waited until Maria turned back from the nightstand. Maria held her hands loosely by her folded legs, with her head facing downward in submission.

Olivia silently gently cursed Maria and reached for her again. As Maria responded, Olivia's mind focused on determining whether Maria was making love to her through desire or duty. "This be not well," thought Olivia.

Maria sucked on Olivia's nipples and she gasped in surprise. Olivia remembered where she was and decided to make this easy for Maria. She pushed Maria away gently, and spread apart her thighs.

"Stay." Olivia's mind raced for words. Maria looked up, puzzled.

"What Country, Friends, is This?"

"Touch but the outside," said the countess.

"What you will, my lady."

"Well, inside a little."

This was how they described their desires to each other. Olivia knew, by this method, she would be aroused quickly, and then Maria and her could embrace in slumber.

* * *

As the sun broke over the horizon, Olivia was awakened by the sound of a mob of men thundering up the stairway to her chamber. Over the tumult, she heard Maria's breaths, as her hands lay across Olivia's breasts. Panicking, Olivia tried to get up, but she couldn't move.

From behind her door, she heard the men slam their bodies against her chamber door. Olivia tried to wake Maria, and push her back to her own bed, but her efforts were in vain.

On the third try, the door flew open and the men poured in. Olivia felt the cold morning air suddenly blow across her naked body.

A priest stepped forward; not good Father Topas, but a different man. Olivia blinked and gasped in horror. It was *Conte* Orsino, wearing a priest's habit!

Orsino pointed at her, and loudly condemned her before the other men: A tribade. A fricatrix. An unnatural girl. The men bound Olivia, still naked, in irons and paraded her past the people of her house without clothes or shoes.

Next, Olivia was clothed, but in ragged dirty linen, standing in the back of a peasant's cart through Piscari. Piscari: The town in which she was born. Piscari: The

Twelve Nights with Viola & Olivia

town her family had ruled for centuries. Piscari: The town whose castle had named her family.

Every face Olivia saw, Olivia knew, and each one bore a grimace of anger and fury against her. Those not driven by hatred were gripped by fear; terrified by the disaster that Providence must send against them if they did not remove Olivia from the town, without delay. All must witness their retribution against her.

The people started accompanying their voices with clods of muck, and then stones. In her senseless stupor, Olivia saw the stones flying toward her, but as they struck, she flinched, but she did not feel them.

Suddenly, the cries and jeers rose to a deafening tumult. Olivia turned her head and saw a stake standing in the main square of Piscari, surrounded by bundles of faggots. Olivia shook with horror. A brazier stood next to the stake; in it, coals burned furiously. Olivia looked down and found a rosary. She clutched the crucifix and prayed furiously.

Olivia was still praying when she was bound to the stake. The ropes had been pulled so tight that Olivia could not move her legs. The faggots were lit and the coiling smoke blackened her face. Her long blonde hair caught fire, and her feet started burning. Olivia kissed the rosary and the rising flames flashed before her face. Olivia started screaming. And crying. And shaking. And screaming. And screaming. And screaming.

"My lady, what doth vex thee?"

Maria already had on her dressing gown, as she embraced Olivia, trying to calm her hysterical friend, stop her from shaking and crying in fear. In the process, Maria shook Olivia awake.

"What Country, Friends, is This?"

"My lady, thou dream't another ill dream!" Maria reassured Olivia, stroking her hair as she had done since they were both children. "May that not be an omen," Maria chuckled. Maria did a quick sign of the cross. Like many of that time, Maria thought dreams foretell the future.

"Oh!" gasped Olivia. Her breaths slowed, and her tears stopped flowing.

"Of what did you dream that frightened you so?"

What could Olivia say? The truth was too terrifying to say. For now, and for centuries past, the Church had killed women that loved women as Olivia loved Maria.

Ironies of Ironies: Olivia could kill a man of lesser rank for spite or sport, and the Church might not even protest. But to love Maria, or another girl or woman, could cost Olivia her life.

Olivia lied.

"It was a monster. I dreamt a monster had chase of me."

"You must have seen the Evil One himself!" Maria answered. "Fear not the dark fiend, my lady. Thou art righteous!"

"What did Maria mean, 'thou art righteous?'" thought Olivia. "Does she not know what she does?"

"I will say my prayers," said Olivia with panicked rapidity. "And we shall pray again in the chantry this morn." Maria nodded.

Twelve Nights with Viola & Olivia

And yet, thought Olivia, if their love was pure, how could their touches be sinful? Why was she made to risk so much for Maria's touch?

As she dried her eyes, Olivia revised. Her love for Maria was a sin; a sin too great to absolve or forgive. The weight of her guilt she must bear alone; to even confess it to a priest would betray herself to her executioners. She must cease her evil-doing forthwith.

These nightmares were beyond what she could bear. A moment of worry or a streak of fear, she could wave away with a shake of her head. In a nightmare, her mind conspired against herself, conjuring vivid terrors while her eyes were closed and she could not escape her fear. "Is this how people go mad?" she asked herself.

Perhaps she should marry a man. He would be her life, and she would bear him children. Many children. She would want no other.

Resolved: She must embrace a suitor. She must find a suitable man for marriage. She must not delay this too long.

Olivia felt Maria's embrace with the warmth of the rising sun.

Yet her love for Maria was too deep, too genuine, too joyous, too warm to be sinful. How could God have made Maria's touch feel so good that she could not live without her? Olivia reached up to share a kiss with Maria.

What man feels as soft and smells as sweet as Maria? What man's voice is as gentle as music from a wood pipe? Not a one. Moreover, Maria was a virtuous maid, not given to drunkenness or lechery like her uncle Tobi.

"What Country, Friends, is This?"

"Maria!" The sound of her name sounded a chord in her heart. This must be love. True love. Even love without a man. Better than love with a man.

Olivia checked that her chamber door was still barred. It was. Of course, it was; she had not yet dressed.

"I do so love you!" Olivia said softly to Maria.

At that moment, Olivia could not imagine a life with any other than Maria; and Maria would do anything to protect her dear precious *Contessa* Olivia.

Chapter Two

"Thy Constellation is Right Apt"

Across the valley of the Piscari from Olivia's estate, *Conte* Orsino strode forcefully amongst his gentlemen.

"Who saw Cesario, ho?" he asked.

The men looked around them, for that name was yet unfamiliar to them. A soft, thin, melodic voice pierced the din, with a hesitant, yet clear answer:

"On your attendance, my lord."

A slight and diminutive figure stepped forward and cautiously bowed to Orsino. The Count warmly placed his arm around Cesario and drew him away. When they were out of earshot, the Count spoke to his youngest gentleman.

"Cesario: Thou knoweth no less than all. To thee, hath I unclasped the book of my soul," said Orsino, who fancied himself a natural poet.

"Ay, my lord."

"Go to She," continued Orsino, in reference to Olivia. "Unfold the passion of my love. She will attend it better in thy youth than a nuncio of grave aspect."

Silently, the youth called "Cesario" immediately foresaw the approaching disaster. For "Cesario" was

Twelve Nights with Viola & Olivia

really Viola, a noble girl of 16 years, pretending to be a boy. Fleeing Turkish-occupied Greece, she had narrowly-survived a shipwreck in a storm ten nights ago. Friendless and alone, she had disguised herself to be able to travel safely while searching for her twin brother Sebastos, if he had also survived the shipwreck.

The thought of speaking words of love to a girl, even as a love-attorney for her lord, was already distasteful for innocent Viola, who had become a boy before considering quite what is expected of a boy.

Viola tried to avoid her duty.

"Sure, my lord, if she be abandoned to sorrow, she'll not admit me."

"Dear lad, believe it! Beshrew they that say thou art a man." Orsino then recited the reasons he had decided to nominate his new young gentleman to be his love-attorney:

"Diana's lip is not more smooth and rubious," said he to Viola. "Thy pipe is as shrill as a maiden's organ." The Count ran his fingers across Viola's soft throat.

"All is semblative in thee a woman's part."

Viola started to suspect that Orsino had already discovered her secret. Orsino continued:

"Prosper well in this, and thou shall live as free as thy lord."

He has no idea who I am, Viola concluded. Without recourse, she agreed.

* * *

Of all the rooms in the Castellamare house, the antechamber was Olivia's favourite, and where she

"Thy Constellation is Right Apt"

received visitors most often. On one side of the room, were windows overlooking and doors leading to a garden that extended to the orchards of the estate. Perpendicular to the garden doors were a window and a smaller door leading to a pergola that ended at the loggia of the house.

On each side of the garden windows were heavy curtains; protective shutters hung on the window frames outside. This morning, they were open to admit light and air into the room.

Arranged around the antechamber were chairs and couches, richly upholstered to provide for the comfort of the person resting upon them. The walls were painted in colors that captured the red in the setting sun. Upon these walls hung portraits of past counts and countesses of the Castellamare line.

In the most honoured place were portraits of Olivia's late father and mother. A portrait of Olivia's late brother stood upon a stand, draped in black silk crepe.

Olivia was with Maria that morning when she was informed that a man of Orsino sought audience. At first, she directed that the man and his attenders be sent away. However, the visitor persisted, and insisted he would remain at her gate until Olivia would see him.

For all her prudence and reserve, Olivia was sometimes given to fancies. When she heard that the new man of the Count was unusually handsome and very young, a combination of curiosity and desire reminded Olivia of her resolution to make a suitable marriage. "A look can do no harm," she thought.

"Give me my veil. We'll once more hear Orsino's embassy," she commanded her servants.

Twelve Nights with Viola & Olivia

Olivia smiled to Maria as she often did when she had spun a new plan. When she saw that particular smile, Maria frowned, knowing Olivia could be capricious and rash. Still, Maria kept her counsel and duly obeyed Olivia.

Maria obediently arranged Olivia's mourning veil to conceal her face while her favourite servants, Rosaline and Lavinia, closed the curtains to shut out the sun. Shut from light and the outside air, the room became somber as a tomb. Rosaline took up her place to play music as Lavinia lit candles with a taper.

Only after they had adjusted the cloth around the picture of Olivia's brother, and Rosaline began to play a *Lamentatio*, was Viola finally admitted.

Viola entered the room and saw several figures, all dressed in black. One woman played a sad tune on a viola da gamba, while three other women sat silently. The tallest figure sat with her back to the door from which Viola entered. Through the veil upon the lady's head, Viola saw that her hair was flaxen blonde, in contrast to the brunette shades of the other maidens.

As Viola stepped forward, the musician stopped. Viola cleared her throat and spoke. In the perfect silence, Viola's voice seemed to shatter the space.

"The honourable lady of the house, which is she?"

"Speak to Me: I shall answer for her," declared the blonde figure. Her irritation was as palpable as her nobility.

Viola stepped closer, reviewed Orsino's love-poem, cleared her throat and began to speak. Olivia refused to turn her head to acknowledge her visitor.

"Thy Constellation is Right Apt"

"Most radiant, exquisite and unmatchable beauty…" Viola began.

"Whence came you, sir?" Olivia interrupted, while she continued to stare angrily at the curtains.

"I have studied, but I can say little more," answered Viola. "Good gentle one, assure me that you are the lady of the house, that I may on with my speech."

The soft music of Viola's voice played upon Olivia's ears like falling showers upon her garden. Olivia was intrigued, and turned toward Viola.

"Are you a comedian?"

Upon seeing Olivia's face, and her inquisitive eyes, Viola felt more at ease; she made a brave face.

"No, my profound heart. And yet, I am not what I play," Viola confessed. "Are you the lady of the house?"

Olivia responded firmly: "If I do not usurp myself, I am!"

"Then I will on with my speech in your praise, and then show you the heart of my message," Viola proposed.

"Come to what is important in it. I forgive you the praise," huffed Olivia.

"My lady, I took pains to study it. 'Tis poetical."

"More like it be feigned," scoffed Olivia. "I pray you, keep it in."

Maria saw her chance to separate the two youths; she walked to Viola, placed her hand on her shoulder, and pointed to the hallway door.

"Will you hoist sail, sir? Here lies your way!"

Twelve Nights with Viola & Olivia

Viola pulled her shoulder from Maria's grip.

"No, good swabber. I will hull here a little longer." Viola turned back to Olivia, and spoke softly: "Tell me your mind: I am a messenger."

"Surely you have some hideous matter to deliver, when the courtesy of it is so fearful," said Olivia. "What are you? What would you?"

"My lady," began Viola, "What I am, and what I would, are as secret as maidenhead." Viola fought an urge to wink at her own innuendo.

Instead, Viola leaned close enough to Olivia's veil that she stared tunnels into the eyes of the countess. Viola continued, in the same soft – and for Olivia, seductive – voice: "To your ears, divinity; to any other's: profanation."

Sitting so close to Viola, Olivia felt the same tingling she felt when she and Maria were alone together. For a moment, she felt utterly unable to control herself. "What a man can do to me!" she marvelled.

Olivia smiled at Viola as the count's love-attorney backed away. She ordered Maria and her other servants: "Give us this place – alone." Olivia said that last word firmly to leave no doubt. Olivia feigned sarcasm: "We will hear this 'divinity.'"

Maria stared at Olivia with disapproval, then led the other ladies from the room. Loud enough so that Olivia heard it, Maria closed the door. Olivia stared at Viola; happy that her veil concealed that she was blushing.

Viola was the first to break the silence.

"Most sweet lady—"

"Thy Constellation is Right Apt"

Olivia threw down her shoulders, and sighed in irritation. "Oh, sir! Have you no more to say?"

Viola remembered that Orsino had asked his love-attorney to verify the beauty of the countess.

"Good madam, by the will of my lord, may I see your face?"

"Orsino commissioned you to appraise me?" said Olivia. "Very well: We will draw the curtain and show you the picture."

Olivia turned her back to Viola while she carefully removed her veil, and used her fingers to restore the natural waves in her hair. With her back still to Viola, Olivia jested upon her looks:

"Look you sir: Such a one I was this present: Is't not well done?"

When Olivia turned to face Viola, she nearly gasped from surprise. "He is a wonder!" thought Olivia. The countess thanked herself for allowing herself to see the boy an obstruction to her view.

Viola announced what she would report to Orsino:

'Tis beauty truly blent, that Nature's hand has laid upon."

Olivia blushed, while remarking on the lad's poetic skill. Helplessly, she brought her face not a hands-breadth from Viola's lips before conquering her will to kiss them. Resolved, she ran to the garden windows, drew away a curtain and opened the door that it covered.

"Come sir, with me."

Twelve Nights with Viola & Olivia

Olivia entered her garden, and let her face draw in the warm Abruzzi sunshine. Still astonished, Viola ran to catch up to her. Viola bent her voice to express the depth of Orsino's desire for Olivia:

"My lord and master loves you: O, that such love could be recompensed."

Olivia sighed; Orsino was not the one that she sought to love. She stopped and turned to make her point firmly.

"Your lord knows my mind: I cannot love him."

Olivia shook her head with exhaustion. "He might have took his answer long ago."

The count's love-attorney pleaded the case of the Count:

"If I did love you in my master's flame, in your denial I would find no sense!"

Now this was a topic that could interest Olivia. She spoke in her most doting voice.

"Why? What would you?"

Viola's mind scrambled to imagine how a man might demonstrate his devotion to a beloved girl.

"I'd—I'd make a willow cabin at your gate."

"Oh?" Olivia smiled.

"And—Call upon your soul within the house."

Olivia nodded with appreciation.

"Halloo your name to the reverberate hills." Viola's mind started to roll like incoming breakers.

"Thy Constellation is Right Apt"

Olivia grinned at the show Viola was giving. Her smile made Viola think she was winning her heart, which she was.

"I'd make the—the babbling gossip of the air cry out: Olivia!"

"Beshrew me, the youth's a rare courtier!" she thought. In her mind, Olivia entertained that the youth was expressing his feelings for her, a boy she already loved.

"Lady, you should not rest between the elements of air and earth: But you should pity me!"

Olivia applauded Viola while beaming with joy. The eyes of her ladyship were as bright as beacons. Viola fought the urge to dance in celebration. She had broken into the marble breast of the countess!

Olivia was in love with the boy. She was glad they were in the garden, where they could be observed; out here, she could resist kissing him.

Olivia glanced up to see Maria looking down upon her from the second floor of the house; The present thoughts of her chambermaid did not appear to be happy ones, but she would explain later.

Yet even in her first blush of infatuation, Olivia still had enough sense to remember her obligation to not marry a man that would harm the position of her family. She must know more about this boy!

"Good sir, what is your parentage?"

Viola could afford to reveal little. "Above my fortunes, yet my state is well. I am a gentleman."

Twelve Nights with Viola & Olivia

Olivia tried to understand what Viola had said: Is he saying that his father was a count but he isn't? What shift of fortune could cause his father to fall so?

Viola interrupted the thoughts of the countess.

"My lady, what shall I tell my master?"

Olivia's heart broke as she sensed the boy's increasing disappointment and discomfort:

"Get you to your lord: I cannot love him; let him send no more."

Viola nodded slowly to signal her understanding.

"Unless—perchance—you come here again."

Viola's eyes betrayed her rising panic, but Olivia ignored it.

"Then you can tell me how he takes it."

Viola nodded and backed away in haste.

"I—I must away. My lord will want me."

Olivia nodded with sorrow. In her panic, Viola began to curtsy, then remembered to bow. She walked away, but fought the urge to run from Olivia. Viola left by a gate and found her way out.

Olivia sighed and returned to the ante-chamber, and hastily removed a ring from her finger. As Olivia entered the house, she passed her ladies as they re-entered the room. Olivia continued into the hallway, trailed by Maria, who recognized when the countess was resolved.

Olivia found her messenger, a slight young man.

"What Ho, Adriano!"

Adriano bowed swiftly.

"Thy Constellation is Right Apt"

"Here madam, at your service."

Olivia feigned a state of cold fury.

"Adriano: Take this ring. Run after that same— peevish messenger, the county's man." Olivia flipped a well-trimmed arm toward Orsino's house.

Adriano nodded while Maria relaxed.

"Give it to him: Tell him I'll none of it!"

Adriano took the ring and began to bow. Maria nodded with satisfaction.

"But should he come tomorrow, I'll— I'll give him reasons."

Adriano bowed slowly to show his respect, but Olivia was impatient.

"Hie thee, Adriano!"

Adriano walked swiftly to the front door; once outside, he started running. As Maria saw Adriano leaving, she enjoyed her feeling of satisfaction: Olivia had dismissed the messenger of the Count.

Soon, Maria would suspect she was mistaken.

* * *

Adriano did not have to run long to catch sight of Viola.

"Hold, Noble Sir!" he shouted.

Viola turned and recognized the livery of the countess upon her interceptor. She waited for Adriano to reach her.

"God save you, sir!" greeted Adriano, with a bow.

"And you too, sir!" answered Viola.

Twelve Nights with Viola & Olivia

"I am a messenger of Lady Olivia," began Adriano, as he held out Olivia's ring. "Sir, it is my duty to return this ring to your lordship. She bids you to put him into desperate assurance she will none of him."

Viola's face lost colour and she fought her urge to panic. Adriano grabbed her hand and pushed the ring onto her middle finger.

"Ah, sir: It fits your hand well," mused Adriano.

Viola angrily pulled back her hand. "And what of that?"

"Nothing sir," Adriano said, trying to mollify the count's love-attorney.

"I gave her no ring, sir!" Viola insisted.

"Faith," replied Adriano. "Perchance she loves you, sir."

"This cannot be!" exclaimed Viola in a girlish shriek devoid of her masculine pretence. Then, remembering her place, Viola calmed herself.

"I mean, I cannot have her," she said to Adriano.

"It's all one to me, Sir" he replied. "She bids you return on the morrow. You may tell her then."

Viola removed the ring and held it out.

"Good sir, take this ring off me and bring it to her," Viola pleaded.

Adriano shook his head. "Nay sir, it's not worth her displeasure to me."

Adriano leaned toward Viola and lowered his voice.

"Thy Constellation is Right Apt"

"Mind you, sir. If she wills, take her. She's the fairest maid in the duchy."

"This, I shall tell my lord."

"She's the ripest peach in the orchard, sir. Pluck her while you can."

Viola shook her head in bewilderment. "Is't possible?"

"Sir, hath you more for my lady?"

Viola let her curiosity get away from her.

"Good sir, what are you?" asked Viola. For from the moment that she had heard seen Adriano approach, Viola thought she was seeing a girl of twenty or so years dressed as a man.

"Oh, mayhaps you think I counterfeit a maiden," began Adriano. "Nay sir, I am only what Nature wouldst I be," he explained. Viola nodded. "A man, with the pipe of a maid, and much of her outside."

"Most wonderful!" appreciated Viola. Then, catching herself, she lowered her voice: "Wouldst I say, were I a maiden."

"I hath served her ladyship for half-score years," Adriano continued. "She pitied me whence seeing boys beat me after school."

"Lady Olivia: She is kind?" asked Viola.

"Most definitely, sir," Adriano said as he nodded, before reaching out and squeezing Viola's bicep muscle.

"A fit man, you are," appreciated Adriano. "Sir, she wills that you return anon. God save you."

Twelve Nights with Viola & Olivia

Adriano bowed and Viola nodded weakly. Adriano turned and walked toward Olivia's house. Viola stood holding the ring, staring into its jewels and filigree, as though the ornament held the answers to her questions.

"What means this lady?" thought Viola. As much as the thought horrified her, she was all but certain that Olivia was in love with her. By her one fateful gift, Olivia had pledged to Viola a love as enduring and constant as the circumfrence of the ring in her hand.

"Why?" Viola asked herself. "What does she see in me?" Viola judged her body so slight and weak, compared to boys, that she marvelled her frolic had endured even this long.

Viola paused to watch Adriano's slight frame disappear from her view. "He saith Olivia is kind," recalled Viola. Viola sat upon a nearby boulder to ponder.

Viola remembered that, after surviving the shipwreck, she had proposed to ask Olivia for help the moment she learned her name: She had thought the countess would pity a fellow maiden and assist her. Only after she was told Olivia had cloistered herself to mourn her brother, had she decided to approach the house of Orsino.

Now she knew Olivia's doors were open to her. Viola even held a ring symbolizing Olivia's enduring love for her. "She loves Me!" exclaimed Viola.

"Yes," continued Viola in her thoughts, "Olivia hath given me this ring thinking I am man. She shall take back her love once I reveal to her, sure."

"Yet what if she doesn't?" Viola asked herself. She recalled their recent meeting, and how Olivia had smiled

"Thy Constellation is Right Apt"

constantly, as though she knew an amusing secret. "Mayhaps," thought Viola, "she knows I am a maid; still she wants me!"

"Lady Viola is kind," Adriano had said. Yes, but Viola had sensed a certain madness in the countess. In all Abruzzi, Viola had no friends but Orsino and his men. On the other hand, Olivia was not a one that accepted denials, Viola was sure.

"She may have me, no matter what I will," Viola perceived. "Then, I shall be undone!"

There was nothing for it: She must return to Orsino.

At any event, Viola thought, if she valued her head, Orsino must not know the present object of Olivia's love.

"Is she mad?" Viola asked again of Olivia. "Does she not know what Orsino may do?" For as much as Viola had come to like Orsino, the *Conte* had his dark moods: He could destroy them: Both Olivia and the unfortunate unhappy she had snared.

Viola started planning what she would say to Orsino. She knew already what she would keep from him.

* * *

Had Viola known more about the laws of the land to which she had come, she would have known that the Church had long decreed that any girl or woman that dressed as a man may forfeit her life. Moreover, if she, while pretending to be a man, were found to have lain with another girl or woman, death for both was nearly certain.

Without knowing it, with pure innocence and good intentions, Viola had committed a crime for which she might lose her body and condemn her soul. With equal

Twelve Nights with Viola & Olivia

innocence, Olivia had signed a warrant of death for them both. Only the coming nights and days would decide whether their bodies would be set ablaze as Olivia had dreamt that very morning.

Chapter Three
"If ever Thou shall Love, Remember Me"

Later that day, Olivia sat with Maria in the vine-covered pavilion on the far side of her inner garden, taking their daily *riposo*. Chastely, they leaned against each other, touching shoulders as two close friends. As Olivia tried to nap, Maria knitted.

However, today Maria sensed that Olivia was more restive than resting. She set down her knitting and caught Olivia's eyes with hers.

"Yes, Maria?" said Olivia, expecting an inquiry from her gentlewoman.

"Your will, my lady?" asked Maria.

Olivia considered her words, then spoke.

"Maria, thy pardon for not asking thou ere this present."

"Ay, my lady."

Olivia scanned the area around for eavesdroppers before speaking to Maria.

"I do love thee."

"That I know," said Maria. "And you have all my love, withal."

Twelve Nights with Viola & Olivia

Olivia paused again to choose her words. "Perchance thou hast noted some inconstancy in my—"

Maria swept in to rescue Olivia: "Art you in love?"

"I don't— Mayhaps—" Olivia sighed her defeat. "Yes," she confessed.

"Vex not, my lady," began Maria. "Long have I a-waited this day."

Her response surprised Olivia. "Thou take it well, Maria."

"My lady, doth you recall what Sophia, your mother, said of us?" asked the gentlewoman.

"She said many things."

"She said we went like Juno's swans, so were we inseparable."

Olivia nodded, remembering her beloved late mother. "She did presage we should be together always."

"Wouldst thou let me serve thee; never shall we part."

Olivia leaned toward her gentlewoman. "O Maria!" She said. "I would not wish any companion but thee." Discreetly, Maria squeezed Olivia's hand.

"Whence Leonato, your brother, was no more to protect you," began Maria, "twas then you made known you would see no man."

"No man was more dear to me than my brother."

"Yes, truly," acknowledged Maria. "Yet, I did not foresee you would fulfil your vow."

"Wherefore, Maria?"

"If ever Thou shall love, Remember Me"

"You must have a son for your line, my lady," said Maria. "I have sense to know I cannot forever have thee alone."

Seeing tears in Olivia's eyes, Maria tried to change the subject. "My lady, be there one upon whom your favour falls?"

"Thou will think me a fool," Olivia blushed.

'Tis the county's man, is't?" asked Maria.

"Didst I betray myself?" asked Olivia.

Maria pointed to Olivia's hand. "That finger had a fine ring upon it this morn."

"Thou must think me a fool," Olivia confessed.

"There art much to recommend him," Maria assessed. "He shall take the bit well." Maria chuckled.

Maria's joke shocked Olivia, as she thought herself pliant to men. "Doth thou not think I shall be a proper wife?"

"Your pardon, my lady; I jest," Maria apologized. "Yet such a youth will wear to thee; may fortune shine upon you."

* * *

On her return, Viola reported her love-attorney performance to an anxious Orsino.

As for Olivia's ring: She kept that secretly concealed in her purse.

After supper, Orsino took his new gentleman "Cesario" aside. Viola was surprised at the remarkable friend she had made so quickly. Less than a fortnight ago had she

Twelve Nights with Viola & Olivia

been pulled from the sea onto the shores of this foreign land. Now she was a companion to the local ruler.

All day, after "Cesario" had returned from Olivia, the Count had noticed his new gentleman had been uncharacteristically distracted, as though overwhelmed by thoughts and desires. To the love-sick count, the cause was clear.

"Cesario," began the Count, "thine eye hath strayed upon some favour that it loves: Hath it not?"

The tenderness of the Count stirred Viola's fugitive love for him.

"A little, by your favour," Viola admitted.

"What kind of woman is't?"

Viola thought quickly. "Of your complexion, sir."

Orsino shook his head with disapproval. "She is not worth thee, then. What years, i'faith?"

"About your years, my lord," said Viola.

Orsino chuckled and slapped Viola on her back. "Too old, by heaven!" Then like a co-conspirator, he told her: "My boy, women are as roses, whose fair flower, doth fall that hour!"

Viola forced a laugh, knowing that her own bloom would soon fade. The Count interpreted the reluctance of "Cesario" as a courtier's modesty, and turned to another subject pressing upon his mind.

"Thou saith Olivia wills thy return."

"Ay, my lord. That says she."

"Thou shall go," Orsino directed. "Get thee to yond same cruelty."

"If ever Thou shall love, Remember Me"

Viola remembered Olivia's ring. A flash of panic crossed her. "This cannot be!" thought Viola.

"But if she cannot love you, sir?" Viola asked desperately.

Orsino replied decisively: "I cannot be so answered!" The passion of his outburst surprised other men nearby.

"Sooth, but you must!" said Viola, before pleading her own reckless case.

"Say sir, that some lady – as perhaps there is – hath for your love so great a pang as you have for Olivia."

"Yes?" answered Orsino.

"Wouldst you have her?"

"Lad, no other woman of noble birth lives here," said Orsino, in error.

"Yet, I know—"

"What dost thou know?"

"Perchance you quit your hunt for Olivia—" began Viola, already imagining herself revealing herself to Orsino.

"Ay?"

"I will bring her to you in the morrow," vowed Viola.

Orsino recalled the residents of Olivia's house. "Wouldst thou ally me with her *Nobildonna*?"

"Nay, my lord."

Orsino shook his head. "Youth: I am resolved for Olivia."

Twelve Nights with Viola & Olivia

"By my troth, sir: Another shall cherish you," insisted Viola.

Orsino questioned Viola. "Be she fair as Olivia?"

"Not as fair, my lord," said Viola, doubting her looks.

"She is not worth me. Perchance she is ripe as Olivia?" referring to the readiness of the countess for children.

Again, Viola nodded: "Not as so ready."

"I must have a son. And her station must sure be below the countess."

"Ay." Viola pleaded: "But sir, shouldst you deny her, she may be undone! How can she be answered?"

Viola's pleas touched the sympathetic heart of Orsino: "Boy, when next thou see her, tell her this: I will join her to a proper man."

"In faith, she shall hear it."

"Cesario: On the morrow, go to her."

* * *

As Viola prepared to leave Orsino's house the next morning, a young gentleman entered Piscari town. At least for this province, his clothes were in style, although not quite suited for a noble as he was. On his belt and baldric, he bore a rapier and a dagger, both sheathed.

Though still a boy, he stood as tall as Viola and his hair was the same colour and length. His face bore her noble features. His eyes were just as lively, although his muscles were more developed. He was Viola's identical twin. He was Sebastos.

New to Piscari, Sebastos walked slowly past the market stalls and the shops of artisans. He took note of

"If ever Thou shall love, Remember Me"

the wares on sale, for soon he would need provisions for a passage to Padua, where he would tell his uncle Angelino that his sister had been lost on their crossing of the sea. In Padua, he hoped to also find his mother Elena, safe after her own travels.

Sebastos sensed a man approaching behind him. When he turned, he could not believe his eyes.

"Well met, sot!" cried Sebastos. It was Antonio, the man of two score years who had rescued him from the sea. For more than a week, he had given him food and drink, sheltered him, and shared his bed. Once Sebastos had recovered, Antonio had given him his best clothes, weapons, and enough money to make passage to Padua. All this time while Sebastos hid his ancestry with a lie.

"Roderigo, I couldst not stay behind: My desire for you did spur me forth," said Antonio.

Sebastiano owed Antonio his life, and he knew the man before him risked his life every moment he strayed near the presence of Orsino. For both their sakes, he willed that Antonio return to his home.

"Sir, you saved my life once; for me, risk not yours again."

Antonio discounted the threat upon his head. "The matter of which I spoke is not so grave."

"Ay, but—"

"Nor is yours to be sought."

Sebastos decided that, if he could not slip from Antonio, he must tell him how he came to Abruzzi.

Twelve Nights with Viola & Olivia

"Let us then to a tavern, where I will tell you wherefore came I here."

"To the Elephant!" said Antonio, naming a place nearby.

"I do remember," replied Sebastiano, as Antonio had named it his favourite haunt in Piscari, before the war.

The Elephant stood off the main square, close to the harbour. In the evenings, it was always crowded and loud. This morning, the place was almost empty.

Sebastos and Antonio seated themselves at a table in the courtyard of The Elephant.

Today, Sebastos had resolved to start to go by the Italian version of his name.

"Noble Antonio, your pardon as was I false to you. I am not a Roderigo. In my country I am Sebastos, but here call me Sebastiano. My father was Sebastos also, he too of Messaline," naming his home province in Greece.

"Tis a land I know," replied Antonio, the sturdy ship captain. "The heathen Turks have it now."

"Those same Turks did slay him, sir." Sebastos's voice shook with unquenched fury.

"He left behind my mother and his issue: Myself and a sister, both born in an hour: Yet so might we have ended!"

"Jove, deny it!" exclaimed Antonio.

"But you sir, altered that. Yet before you took me from the sea, was my sister drowned."

"Alas, the day!"

"A lady, sir, though like to me, was accounted beautiful," said Sebastos as he choked his tears. "She is

"If ever Thou shall love, Remember Me"

drowned sir, with salt water: With that, I remember her more."

Antonio solemnly raised his goblet. "To your sister, Sebastiano. May her soul be at peace." Sebastiano raised his goblet to share the toast.

"We were bound, us two, to Padua, where lives an uncle."

"Divers Greeks hath the Turks driven there."

"Now you know why must I set course for Padua."

Antonio patted Sebastiano's shoulder. "Lad, I will find us a ship bound there."

Sebastiano recoiled with surprise. "We sir? 'Tis enough to help me find a ship, for which, my eternal thanks."

"I have friends in the Veneto. Before my ship was taken, oft I sailed with my crew to its ports," related Antonio. "You will find me useful as your servant, noble sir."

Sebastiano did not want Antonio to travel with him, but he also did not want to give him offense.

"What you think best, noble Antonio," said the gentleman.

Antonio took charge. "Let us eat a good meal here, thence go to the harbour for a ship bound to the Veneto." Sebastiano nodded his agreement.

"After, we may enjoy this town 'til the time of our passage," Antonio proposed.

"Sir, may you find good fortune in the Veneto," wished Sebastiano, raising his goblet.

Twelve Nights with Viola & Olivia

"Lad, the cities of the Republic are a marvel. May fortune smile upon you there."

"I think well of Piscari, sir."

"The Veneto is better for one of your birth. You shall gladly shake the dust of Abruzzi from your heels."

After their meal, Sebastiano and Antonio walked to the harbour to find a ship that would take them to the Veneto. As they walked amongst the ships, Antonio insisted that Sebastiano call him his servant.

Knowing something of the past of his friend, Sebastiano made a brave face, passing himself off as a nobleman—as he was—wanting to journey to the north of Italy, with his trusted servant. Some sailors recognized Antonio, but they hid their knowledge.

At length, they found a good ship bound for Venezia: A caravel with two masts, 20 tons in displacement, and a worthy crew of five. One man Antonio knew. Antonio deemed this vessel fit for sea service. The ship would leave Piscari with the high-tide, late tonight. They must be at quayside by sundown, lest their place be sold to another.

With the price agreed upon, and arrangements made, Sebastiano and Antonio went to the market square to purchase provisions for their voyage.

Chapter Four

"I would Thou were as I would have Thee be!"

Minutes after Sebastiano and Antonio entered The Elephant, Viola walked through the market square toward the house of Olivia. When she arrived, she was swiftly ushered into the garden. Olivia was no longer in mourning clothes, but dressed in a rose-coloured gown the colour of her cheeks, seated in the pavilion just starting to be warmed by the morning sun.

"Youth, I did send a ring in chase of you," began Olivia. "So did I abuse myself, my servant, and I fear, you." Olivia looked down, fearing Cesario would chastise her.

"What might you think?" she asked.

"My lady—" began Viola, before halting with a sigh.

"Yes, good sir?" asked Olivia, expectantly.

Viola found the right words. "My lady: I pity you."

Olivia raised her head, with hope. "Sure that's at least a degree to love."

Viola shook her head sympathetically. "Nay, my lady. 'Tis a vulgar proof."

She removed Olivia's ring from her doublet pocket and laid it on the table.

Twelve Nights with Viola & Olivia

Olivia pondered the ring in silence. Then, with her characteristic decisiveness, she decided to manifest her wills and wants to this lad.

"Cesario: By the roses of the spring, by maidhood, honour, truth, and everything: I love thee so nay wit nor reason can my passion hide."

Viola shifted Olivia's hands off her body and confronted her.

"By innocence I swear, my lady: I have one heart, that no woman has, nor never none shall be mistress of it!"

Knowing how Olivia's folly could destroy them both, Viola begged her to accept her plea: "Lady, I can never love you."

"I cannot be so answered!" said the countess, unaccustomed to refusal. Viola turned away, pained by her fear of Orsino. The countess interpreted Viola's expression otherwise:

"What a deal of scorn looks comely in the contempt of his lip! A murderous guilt shows itself not more soon than love that has been hid."

Viola wondered if now she should reveal herself. "Nay, lady: Now you will make me your fool!" she protested.

Olivia decided to play her own love-attorney.

"Cesario, am I not fair to thee?" asked Olivia. "I shall stay under roof in sun or rain."

Viola pleaded, "By your favour, nay!"

Olivia shaped her fingers in the gesture that suggests smallness. "I am but a trice above thy years."

"This is a midsummer madness."

"If would Thou were as I would have Thee be!"

Olivia patted her richly-brocaded belly. "And I am ripe, and will breed, by troth!"

Viola nodded, "I trust that true."

"Then what reason for thy deny?" asked Olivia.

Suddenly, a possible explanation entered her mind. "O, sure: Another must be in thine eye!"

"By my honour, nay!"

Olivia interrogated this mysterious gentleman: "Who could she be? Not below thy station!" Viola shook her head.

Caught in her love-madness, Olivia began speaking to herself.

"A duchess, mayhaps. A fair duchess with a jealous father. A father with a murderous wrath." Olivia nodded to herself, without looking at Viola's reactions.

"There's good cause why thou entered this town without history or parentage. Half the town wonders wherefore thou art here. Perchance this answer be true."

While Olivia raved, Viola asked herself: "Wherefore I be here? Hath I not done my duty to my lord? Is it not time for *mio pranzo*? This lady needs no hearer, she provides an audience on her own. 'Tis foul entertainment without compare."

Viola interrupted Olivia's raving. "Nay princess," she said gently. "No woman hath my heart save I alone."

"Yet, perhaps—"

Viola decided to try a sterner approach. "Lady: To know true might cost you dear!"

Twelve Nights with Viola & Olivia

With her quick mind, Olivia immediately guessed the cause of Cesario's fear. "O! Him!" she scoffed with manifest contempt.

"Cesario, fear not: Thou art as great as that thou fear'st."

"That shall I recall at my execution."

Viola repeated her urgings. "My lady, that you think you art, be not what you are!"

* * *

Meanwhile, the Count stood watch on his balcony, peering through his spyglass. Unexpectedly, he had not seen Olivia on her daily ride through the estate. He had also not seen Cesario walking up from Piscari. *Visconte* Curio stood on his attendance.

"He should have returned," Orsino said to Curio. "Fortune forbid he fell not along the way."

Curio nodded, as he also liked the new lad.

"Call forth some officers."

Curio bowed and went inside, while Orsino continued scanning through his spyglass.

* * *

"Dear lad, Orsino is my kin. I shall answer for thee," Olivia assured Viola. "Be not a-feared."

The bell of the clock in Olivia's house struck the hour.

"The clock upbraids me for waste of time."

"Yes, but—"

Making one final attempt, Viola pleaded. "I must have your true love for my master!" Viola pointed toward

"If would Thou were as I would have Thee be!"

Orsino's house. "He will ask me why your demurrer hath taken hours."

Her eyes misted with tears, Olivia shook her head. Viola walked away.

"Yet come again, tomorrow!" Olivia called back. "Perchance thy heart may move to like his love?"

Witnessing Olivia's emotions had made Viola briefly forget her obligations of courtesy. She turned her heels to curtsy, then – after remembering who she was pretending to be – she bowed as gracefully as she could from that awkward position without falling.

* * *

Curio returned to Orsino with two officers.

"Go ye to town, thence to Olivia's house," commanded the count. "Find my gentleman; see he not need some aid."

"Ay, my lord," said the ranking soldier.

"Return with him, or not, as he wills."

"We shall, my lord."

"Go to."

"Ay, my lord."

The officers saluted Orsino, and left.

* * *

Viola left Olivia's garden by the gate through the tall wall that enclosed it. After closing the gate, *Cavaliere* Tobi intercepted her.

"God save you, sir!"

"And you, sir," Viola replied.

Twelve Nights with Viola & Olivia

Tobi placed his hand firmly on Viola's shoulder.

"That defence thou hast, betake to't," Tobi warned. "Thy interceptor, bloody as the hunter, attends thee at the orchard-end." Tobi pointed away from the house.

"You mistake, sir. No man hath quarrel with me."

"You will find it otherwise," Tobi held. "Therefore, come with me, or I will have with you what you might avoid with him." Tobi touched the hilt of his sword. Lacking a better choice, Viola complied.

"Pray you, sir: Do you know of this matter?" asked Viola as he walked with Tobi.

"I know the knight is incensed against you, even to a mortal arbitrement."

"What manner of man is he?" asked Viola.

"He is knight, but a devil in private brawl," answered Tobi. "Souls and bodies hath he divorced: Three." Tobi held up his fingers to emphasize the point.

Already at the orchard, it was too late: Viola saw *Cavaliere* Andreano, practicing his sword-fighting. He was a thin man of about 30 years, who handled his sword coolly, with the ease that comes from decades of regular practice. Viola considered her options: "But a little thing would make me show them how much I lack as a man," she thought.

Suddenly, Adriano passed by. He knew all those present, including Viola. He also knew how much boys delight in hurting boys they deem less manly. Seeing Viola's face filled with fear, Adriano deployed a ruse.

"God save you, sir!" Adriano greeted Viola.

"If would Thou were as I would have Thee be!"

"Pray he does," replied Viola.

"A fair day to practice swordship, your worship."

Viola joined the ruse. "Ay, sir. My best to your lady. Perchance she'd view our fence?" Tobi knew Viola was trying to escape, but he could not stop Adriano, knowing how Olivia would repay him for it.

"Perhaps she will, sir," answered Adriano. "I shall tell her anon." Adriano proceeded to Olivia's house as Viola's eyes followed him.

Tobi turned Viola's head back to the matter at hand. "Courage, lad," said he.

* * *

In her sorrow, Olivia no longer wished to see the sun, and retired to the ante-chamber. There, Maria tried to restore her normal repose. Behind them, the doors were firmly shut.

"Maria: I love him so!" Olivia expressed her frustration. "Why does he not love me?"

"O, poor lady: How Cupid has baffled you!"

"In his denial, I find no sense!"

"My lady, love be not figured like sums," Maria advised. "He cannot love you; you must take your answer."

"Maria, my love is as a fever! Methinks I may die from this plague!"

Maria humorously touched Olivia's forehead. "I trust your love will not claim you so."

Maria tried reason. "Dear lady, the lad has his senses. Many are as be-fuddled by your refusal of the Conte!"

Twelve Nights with Viola & Olivia

A flash of anger streaked across the face of the countess. "O, Fie! Would his thoughts be blanks, than filled with me!" Olivia reminded her gentlewoman: "I bade thee never speak of him."

"Your pardon, my lady. Your reason for denying him is enough for all minds," mollified Maria.

"Desire is like death; which physic does except."

"Perchance he hath given thee cause. Hath he said?"

"Not a grise. He says but: 'He cannot love me.'"

"Wherefore he cannot love you?" delved Maria.

"He says no woman shall have his heart, ever"

Maria pondered Cesario's words. "I have heard—." She stopped, reluctant to continue.

"What hast thou heard?"

"I am chary to say."

"I must know, Maria." Olivia sealed her request with a kiss as her tears fell upon Maria's cheeks. Maria pursed her lips while choosing her words.

"I have heard—" began Maria, softly.

"Yes?" Olivia leaned toward her lover.

"I have heard," said Maria, more strongly, "there are men that would fain have the love of others than women. So have I heard."

"Dost thou mean? Cesario is a—"

At this moment, had Olivia been English, she might have exclaimed: "Oh, bugger!"

"If would Thou were as I would have Thee be!"

Olivia waved away the thought. "Nay, Maria. T'isn't possible."

Maria welcomed the return of Olivia's smile. "Ten ducats, then?" A day's pay for Maria.

"Gold?"

"Ay."

"Done."

"Thou shall lose!" Olivia laughed.

Joining in the fun, Maria declared to her lover, "I'll pay double that to see thee merry!"

Maria and Olivia's revels were disturbed by a knock on the door. Olivia's people knew to only disturb her *riposo* for pressing matters. Maria and Olivia returned to stately poses.

Olivia commanded: "Enter!" Her messenger entered, and hastily bowed.

"My dear Adriano!" for Olivia was fond of her dutiful messenger.

"My lady, I fear yonder youth be in peril."

"Cesario?" asked Olivia.

"Ay, that be his name."

"What's the matter?"

"In the orchard, is he with Tobi and Andreano, swords drawn."

Olivia face immediately manifested fear and anger. "What? In our house?"

Twelve Nights with Viola & Olivia

"Ay. He feigned there would be fence practice," hurried Adriano. "He invited your ladyship to see, but I sensed more."

Olivia's mind raced through the implications.

"We have no battles here! With a man of the Conte?"

Olivia leapt up, furious with her uncle. "Are all these people mad?!"

Seeing Olivia upset pained Adriano. "Madonna—"

"Go to him, sir!" she commanded. "Prithee! Find him! Save him!" she pleaded. "I would not have him miscarry for half my dowry!"

"Fear not, my lady!" Adriano made a hasty bow. "I am away." Knowing the urgency of the moment, Adriano ran toward the orchard.

"Maria!" demanded Olivia, overwhelmed by the moment.

"On your attendance," she answered instantly.

"Go to our wardrobe. We go out anon!"

"What you will, my lady." Skipping the curtsy, Maria rushed to Olivia's chamber.

When she returned, Olivia was adjusting her baldric and belt, from which hung her sword and sheath. Maria's hands went cold.

"My lady!"

"I may have my own bout with Tobi!" snarled Olivia.

Olivia drew her sword with a well-practiced motion. She admired the reflection of light upon the blood groove. She returned the sword to the sheath as adeptly.

"If would Thou were as I would have Thee be!"

Maria's voice shook. "Art you sure that be wise?"

Without a word, Olivia resolutely jutted her head forward, casting toward Maria her most roguish grimace, her eyes spitting fire.

Olivia took her hat from Maria and crushed it upon her head. She kicked off her Venetian slippers without a thought of where they landed, took her boots, and began putting them on her feet.

The look in Olivia's eyes told her that all courtly pretence was for naught. This is no lady, thought Maria; this is a tiger! One as fierce as her father, the count, had been.

The Castellamare blood runs through those veins, she thought. Pray God she spills none today!

Maria readied herself with equal speed to depart with her lady.

Chapter Five

"Make Tempests Kind, and Salt Waves Love!"

Walking past the market stalls, Antonio felt relieved that he would soon leave Abruzzi with his new companion for the opportunities of the Veneto. Although he had used much of his coin to pay for the passage, his traveling companion was a nobleman whose uncle, according to Sebastiano, had established himself in Padua. Soon, thought Antonio, he would be a man of means with young Sebastiano to share his fortunes.

Suddenly, two men of arms approached Sebastiano and saluted.

"Cesario, noble sir," said the officer.

"Gentlemen?" warily answered Sebastiano, knowing that Antonio might be in danger.

"Good day, sir. Your master will be glad you did not miscarry."

Antonio regretted that he was too tall to hide behind Sebastiano.

"My master?" asked Sebastiano. "You mistake me, sir. I am not in service to any man."

"Are you not Cesario, gentleman of the house of Orsino?"

Twelve Nights with Viola & Olivia

"Believe me, sirs," replied Sebastiano. "I know of thy lordship, yet I knew not that other name until you spoke it."

"Troth sir, you are his very reflection."

"Your pardon, that I could not aid you," said Sebastiano. "May you find him, anon."

With that, Sebastiano joined Antonio and walked away.

"Hold, sir! Wait a moment!" called the officer.

With the brusque impudence of one that holds the power of law, the officer knocked Antonio's hat off his head, and pointed at him.

"This is Antonio, the notable pirate!" he declared to his fellow soldier.

"Good sir," pleaded Sebastiano. "You mistake. This is my servant, Roderigo. I love him as my sworn brother!"

"No sir!" replied the officer. "I know his favour well." Turning to his fellow soldier, he ordered: "This is he. Do your office."

"Antonio, I arrest thee at the suit of *Conte* Orsino," said the man. The officer rested his hand upon the hilt of his sword as the soldier bound Antonio's hands with iron shackles. Antonio turned to Sebastiano.

Sebastiano tried his best to persuade the soldiers.

"This is most irregular. I am a gentleman, we leave this place tonight," related Sebastiano. "I give you my word, sir."

The officer paused, remembering the danger of challenging a nobleman, before recalling his duty.

"Make Tempests Kind, and Salt Waves Love!"

"Meddle not, sir; the suit is of the *Conte* himself."

The soldier was kinder, and tried to relieve the nobleman.

"Your favour is an honest one." Then, pointing at Antonio, he said: "I trust this brigand hath told you a tale."

"Know not I for what the *Conte* seeks of him," Sebastiano persisted, "but I must plead for my man."

The officer addressed Sebastiano imperiously. "You may raise his cause at the palace of *Conte* Orsino, sir."

"Ay."

"Any man here knows it," said the officer, motioning to the gathering crowd.

"You will find your friend in the gaol as a guest of his lordship!"

The officer laughed as one who has triumphed over a personal enemy. Members of the crowd cheered the officer and jeered Antonio, as they too had lost friends in the recent small war.

The soldier pulled Sebastiano aside to explain his commander.

"Pardon him, sir. He has personal cause against your friend. And we have still to find the man of the *Conte* for whom we were sent. But then," motioning to Antonio, "we will bring him to his cell."

Sebastiano thanked Jove that he had found a just man in Piscari. "To Orsino's palace; I shall plead for you," he told Antonio. Antonio nodded in response.

"Tarry not, lest you find him not!" The officer laughed.

Twelve Nights with Viola & Olivia

To vigorous cheers from the townspeople, Orsino's men led Antonio away. "I will save you!" Sebastiano called out to his new sworn brother. With the excitement over, the crowd started to disperse. Sebastiano approached the nearest stall-keeper.

"Good sir, know you how I should go to Orsino's palace?" Sebastiano asked.

"Ay, noble sir," said the seller. "Let me get pen and ink and draw that for you. Anon, sir."

As he waited for the merchant to return, Sebastiano felt an unexpected tap on his shoulder. He turned to view the most remarkable-looking young man he had ever seen. It was Adriano.

"Jove be praised! You art safe!" rejoiced Adriano.

"More matter for a May morning," mused Sebastiano.

"Good day to you, sir. And you are called—?"

"Adriano, sir. We met the day a-fore."

"Did we so?"

"Be you not Cesario, the *Conte*'s gentleman?"

"Nay, sir. But the sport is favoured," Sebastiano jested. "Two men of the *Conte* seek him also."

This news displeased Adriano. "O! Mayhaps the *Conte* has heard of the trouble. Well," he assured Sebastiano, "the matter concerns you not."

"And yet it doth, sir," replied Sebastiano. "I am in haste to the *Conte*, just now."

"Make Tempests Kind, and Salt Waves Love!"

"Well, *alla prossima!*" said Adriano in farewell. He looked again at Sebastiano. "You are his very glass image!"

"I may soon play this Cesario game myself," Sebastiano joshed. "But first, my business."

Adriano left, and Sebastiano returned to waiting for the merchant. He was surprised when a slight man with thinning hair grabbed his arm and spun him around.

"Now sir, have I met you again? There's for you!"

Andreano swung at Sebastiano, but the youth was quick and dodged the blow. Angered at this assault on his gentlemanly dignity, Sebastiano returned the knight's favour. "Why there's for thee, and thee, and thee!" he shouted.

With the third blow, Andreano collapsed upon the street. "Are all the people mad?" shouted Sebastiano.

With no friend to protect him, Sebastiano drew his dagger, ready to repel the next on-comer. The crowd that had gathered stepped back while Sebastiano held out his blade. The seller stood amazed, worried what these noblemen would do to his stall.

Suddenly, Sebastiano felt his wrists gripped by a older, but stronger man. He tried to turn his blade to stab his assailant, but was unable.

"Come, my young soldier," urged Tobi. "Put up your iron: You are well-fleshed."

In the struggle, Sebastiano dropped his dagger. With one final push, he broke free from Tobi. Sebastiano retreated three steps, drew his rapier, and pointed its deadly sharp tip at Tobi.

Twelve Nights with Viola & Olivia

"What would thou now?" said Sebastiano, insulting the older knight. "If thou wouldst tempt me further: Draw thy sword!" The crowd spread into a circle but one or two persons deep, but yards in diameter, to not be caught by a misdirected blade.

Tobi had conciliated enough. Now this impudent youth challenged his honour in the main plaza of the town?

Tobi drew his sword, as Andreano retreated through the crowd. Sebastiano stared at Tobi, pondering whether he should first thrust or slash at the knight.

Suddenly, Sebastiano was struck by a vision: A tall beautiful girl with flaxen hair, dressed in satin dyed pink with madder, passed through the line of onlookers, while holding a rapier drawn from the scabbard banging against her skirt.

Sebastiano realized he was not dreaming when Olivia stood behind Tobi, and held the tip of her sword to the back of her uncle.

As the crowd noticed the presence of their Countess, they knelt in homage to her. Behind Olivia followed *Nobildonna* Maria.

"Hold, Tobi!" commanded the Countess, in a voice as loud and direct as Sebastiano had ever heard from a woman. "On thy life, I charge thee sir: Hold!"

Tobi drew in a long slow breath, took a slow cautious step forward, and sheathed his sword.

Following Tobi's cue, Sebastiano sheathed his sword; then deeming it prudent to follow the commoners, lowered himself upon his left knee and bowed his head as well.

The crowd continued to kneel, but looked up to see what Olivia would do. Tobi turned, and like a schoolboy

"Make Tempests Kind, and Salt Waves Love!"

reprimanded by his teacher, he sought to mollify his enraged niece.

Olivia sheathed her sword and waited for Tobi to speak.

"Madam?"

"Will it ever be thus?" she cried.

Olivia pushed him with all her strength.

"Fit for the mountains and barbarous caves?"

Olivia struck Tobi in his undefended loins. He collapsed to the ground. As he writhed on the ground, Olivia shouted at him: "Out of my sight!"

As Tobi crawled away in pain, Olivia walked to Sebastiano, who trembled as he knelt.

"Arise, Cesario," said Olivia to Sebastiano, in her sweetest voice.

"You mistake me, my lady. Cesario, I am not."

Is how Sebastiano should have answered the Countess, before explaining his presence in her town. Instead, he uttered a weak, but deferential, "My lady."

Olivia gripped Sebastiano's shoulders, pulled him up, embraced him, and then kissed his lips long and hard. After the initial shock, Sebastiano returned Olivia's kiss.

At this unexpected display by the countess, the crowd stood up, applauded, and cheered her and the youth they expected would be the next count.

Maria retrieved her purse and counted coins.

Olivia blushed with embarrassment for what her passions had cost her. She stood before the crowd, grasped the hilt of her sword and cried, "Hath ye no other business?"

The townspeople, remembering the power of Olivia, left as she commanded. Sebastiano stood alone with Olivia, very impressed. Olivia turned to Sebastiano.

"Be not offended, Cesario," she said to him. "Let thy fair wisdom, not thy passion, sway in this uncivil extent against thy peace."

Once again, Sebastiano should have realized that the Countess believed that he was someone that he was not.

Maria approached Olivia and said: "Fortune has favoured you, my lady." She handed the countess ten gold ducats, nearly £20 today,* before rushing to help Sir Toby.

Sebastiano was amazed to see so much money handed over freely.

"That is for—?" he asked.

Olivia looked at the coins in her hand. "Oh, it's nothing. Here!" She handed them to Sebastiano, bewildered by Olivia's unexpected gift.

At this moment, Sebastiano remembered something Antonio had told him: Never let a fair chance for riches pass by.

"Come, sir; I prithee," said Olivia. Sebastiano followed Olivia. Suddenly, the countess knelt to him in homage.

"Wouldst thou rule me?"

---

* In 2023, the gold content of 10 Venetian ducats is worth over $1,500 U.S. dollars.

"Make Tempests Kind, and Salt Waves Love!"

Sebastiano could not have been more shocked. "A moment, by your leave." He turned from her to think.

"Am I mad? What flood of fortune comes to me as this?"

"Or—is the lady mad?"

"Yet if she were mad, she could not sway her house, command this town, take and give back affairs with such a stable bearing, as I perceive she does."

While Olivia waited expectantly, Sebastian went to Maria and Tobi to gain their insight.

"Your ladyship has proposed a thing beyond all reason," he said to Maria.

"Ay," she replied dryly.

"Is your ladyship mad?"

Maria shook her head. "Nay sir!" Then, pointing her at Tobi, she assured Sebastiano: "Madness only touch her kinsmen."

Tobi waved weakly in his embarrassment, to confirm that "She means me."

The impatient countess approached Sebastiano and knelt before him on one knee.

"My lord? My liege: Need more time still?"

Sebastiano said with a chuckle: "Your wish is granted. Madam, I will!"

Olivia rose to her feet. "O say so! – and so be!" she rejoiced, before sealing Sebastiano's promise with a kiss.

"Blame not this haste of mine if you mean well," begged Olivia. "Now go with me into the chantry by;

Twelve Nights with Viola & Olivia

plight me the full assurance of your faith; that my most jealous soul may live at peace."

Then, remembering Cesario's (or Viola's) fear of Orsino, she added: "Vex not, fair youth. We shall conceal it 'till you will it come to note, and thence shall be our festive."

Although intoxicated by the presence of Olivia, Sebastiano remembered his duty to his friend.

"I would vow to you thereby were I not bound to the *Conte* to plead mercy for my friend," disclosed Sebastiano. "Twas where I was bound a-fore your sweet enchantment, lady."

Olivia paused for a moment, and then she shrugged. "The *Conte*? O, him. Well:" she began. "See sir priest for me, I'll see sir count for thee." Sebastiano was still confused.

"The *Conte* is my cousin; your friend shall be free," assured Olivia.

Sebastiano thought, "Lady, your offer is my best today. Let's make our vows, lead me the way!"

* * *

That afternoon, Orsino lay on a couch, nursing a headache too severe for him to wait for sight of Olivia, as he usually did.

Visconte Curio approached; Orsino sensed he had a serious matter to relate.

"Good day, my lord," said Curio.

"What news, sir?" asked Orsino.

"Not good news, my lord."

"Make Tempests Kind, and Salt Waves Love!"

"What be in it?"

"Your gentleman, Cesario," reported Curio, "has raised fists and blade 'gainst two noblemen in the town."

"My gentleman?" asked Orsino of his most tranquil and modest of men. He sat up hastily. "Is he hurt?"

"By all accounts, nay."

Orsino sighed his relief.

"That youth hath quarrelled with Olivia's people," Curio related.

"What cause, sir?"

"That is more than I know, my lord."

"Until more news, then," said Orsino, before relaxing against the couch.

"My lord," began Curio. "Fortune may be in this."

Orsino took note. "How now?"

"To visit Her on a matter of state," noted Curio, "Would be fair grounds for you."

Orsino sat up and realized that, by using this excuse that Fortune had given him, he could see Olivia and speak to her without going through an intermediary.

"Sure she will love me whence she sees how easily I can forgive—to her—an insult upon my house," thought the Count.

"Ay," Orsino nodded, "we concur. Ready a visit to Olivia's house," commanded the Count. "Let us go well-attended."

"As you will, my lord." Curio left to organize the men for their departure.

Twelve Nights with Viola & Olivia

* * *

By the chantry on Olivia's estate, the wedding party of Olivia, Sebastiano, Maria, Adriano, her father's old friend Feste, and Father Topas, quietly celebrated the wedding of the countess.

"A thousand good wishes to ye both," said Adriano.

Olivia, dressed in a blue silk gown to express her fidelity, addressed her friends.

"We are glad ye are with us."

Now that Father Topas had blessed the wedding, Maria decided she must bring Olivia to deal with the troubles brought to the house by her uncle.

"My lady, methinks you must parley with Orsino."

"Parley with him? Perché?" for "Orsino" was the last name she wanted to hear now.

"Your kin Tobi, my lady. That other *Cavaliere* hath also trespassed."

"Maria is right, my lady," supported Feste. Thou shouldst be-front thy house to the *Conte*."

"Where is Tobi, now?" asked Olivia.

"My lady, I shall find thy kinsman," offered Feste.

"Good sir, go to Tobi. Fetch him for me." He left.

Olivia vowed: "We shall right this ship." She sighed heavily, as she often did when required to fulfil an infelicitous duty.

"Let us repair to the house and ready our embassy," she told her friends. Then to Adriano she added, "Give

"Make Tempests Kind, and Salt Waves Love!"

word to the Count we seek audience." Upon her command, he bowed and left for Orsino's palace.

At the mention of Orsino, Sebastiano spoke: "As for my friend—"

Olivia turned to her new husband. "O, my sweet one. Ay, thou shall too be with our party."

"To the house, then; at once!" commanded Olivia.

* * *

After outracing Tobi and Andreano, two older men without her ample stamina, Viola threaded the back streets of Piscari before climbing the hill to Orsino's home. Still looking for pursuers, she was surprised to see a cloud of dust ahead of her materialize into a troop of Orsino's soldiers under colourful banners. At the lead rode Orsino and Curio on magnificent steeds.

When the column reached Viola, she removed her cap, and bowed.

"Your most serene lordship!"

Orsino was stern. "Cesario, thou hast raised our displeasure 'gainst thee."

Viola was shocked; she felt her hands grow cold with fear. Barely lifting her head, she meekly asked him: "Sir?"

"Clashing with Olivia's people?" charged Orsino. "Boy, I sent thee to carry words of love, not make a war."

"My lord, I raised no quarrel with them!" pleaded Viola. "Olivia's men gave me challenge and drew upon me; for cause I know not. But with wits and legs did I escape."

"Speak not false to thy lord, sirrah," censored Curio. "We have heard different!"

Twelve Nights with Viola & Olivia

Orsino nodded his agreement.

"That is all I know, my lord." Viola shook her head.

Orsino motioned to the column he led. "Thou shall walk with us in the last rank," he commanded.
"Anon, shall thy fate be set," warned the Count.

At that moment, Viola wanted to run, and run, and keep running until she reached a place where no one knew the names of Orsino or Olivia. However, as though in a dream, she felt unable to run. Viola went to the end of the column as she had been ordered, and trailed the last man, walking like a prisoner.

* * *

In Olivia's house, her people hustled about, with Sebastiano by her side.

"Have my best horses readied for us," she commanded. "We shall make a show of it."

Olivia asked Sebastiano, "Canst you ride, sir?"

"Ably, princess; may I so say. However," caveated Sebastiano, "wouldst we not tarry longer, lest greater misfortune be-fall my friend?"

Olivia reassured Sebastiano: "We shall leave presently, in good order."

An older man in a somber-coloured doublet and a large set of keys at his waist approached Olivia unexpectedly, to raise a matter to which the countess had to attend without delay. Before she left with her *maggiordomo*, Olivia grabbed Fabian, her chief gardener, pointed at Sebastiano, and commanded: "Sir, take horses and lead this man to Orsino's house, at once."

"Make Tempests Kind, and Salt Waves Love!"

Fabian bowed to Olivia. "As you will, my lady."

Olivia assured Sebastiano, "Fabian will lead the way. I shall join thee anon."

Olivia kissed Sebastiano long and deeply, surprising Fabian and most of her people. She then followed her head servant, trailed by the rest of her attendants. Suddenly, Fabian and Sebastiano were alone. Sebastiano spoke first.

"Sir, we must leave with no delay!"

"Verily, we shall. Yet one thing to which I must first attend," said Fabian.

"Sir, the matter is grave."

"Ay, sir. Follow me," replied Fabian.

As they walked toward the garden, Sebastiano—who was starting to panic over the danger facing Antonio—thought he might bring Fabian to take him to horses if he communicated the gravity of the situation.

"Tell me, sir," said Sebastiano. "How soon is a man hung in Piscari?"

Chapter Six

"Long Live the Countess!"

When the countess was finally ready to leave, just one more bell of her clock would sound before sunset. Before she could mount her mare, Olivia first heard, then saw, Orsino's armed column.

"O, what fresh hell is this?" she muttered.

Releasing the reins to an attendant, she ordered her servants: "Lead away the horses. Bring refreshments for us and Orsino!"

On his mighty steed, Orsino was surprised to see Olivia waiting, as though she was expecting him. The still love-struck count joyously remarked to Curio: "Behold, sir: There She is! Now heaven walks the earth."

As Orsino dismounted, Olivia, Maria, and the rest of Olivia's people curtsied and bowed to the noble count. As Orsino's horse was led away, Olivia addressed her ruler.

"What would my lord, but that he may not have, wherein Olivia may be serviceable?" she asked.

"Gracious Olivia—" Orsino began, before Olivia spied Viola, trying to hold her face from the countess. With one gracious hand, she halted Orsino.

"Good, my lord—"

Olivia walked quickly to the last rank of Orsino's men. Orsino followed, surprised by Olivia's action. Maria trailed the Countess out of duty.

Twelve Nights with Viola & Olivia

Olivia was sharp with Viola.

"Cesario, wherefore art thou here? You do not keep promise with me!"

Viola answered with surprise. "Madam?" Curio and Maria joined the count.

"My lady, I beseech thee," implored Orsino, "let me charge my man; he shall soon feel a greater warmth than now, i' faith."

A still-angry Orsino told Viola: "I should let her strike thee, boy!"

"What say thee, Cesario?" Olivia pressed.

"My lord would speak; my duty hushes me," replied Viola.

"Why dost thou speak to my gentleman so?" asked Orsino. "What injury he hath done, I shall answer for it."

Olivia nodded. "My lord, I too shall answer for that outrage by my people, she said. "We want no war with your noble house."

"Yet know you this, sir: I did sure draw on my kin so that your man be not hurt."

Olivia's words puzzled Viola as much as her hand on her cheek annoyed her. "I wouldst not ever see thee hurt," she told Viola.

Orsino drew himself up. "My lady, I must be round with you: We suspect an infamy!"

"My lord," Olivia protested, "there is no treason in it!" Orsino's face and words darkened.

"Why should I not – had I the heart to do it – kill what I love? A savage jealousy that sometimes savours nobly."

"Long Live the Countess!"

"But," Orsino confronted Olivia, "hear me well: Lady!"

Orsino pointed at Viola, who was trying to sink through the surface of the earth.

"This minion, whom I know you love: Him will I tear from that cruel eye," pointing at Olivia. Orsino began to lead Viola away from Olivia.

"Where goes Cesario?" demanded the Countess.

Viola turned to Olivia, to finally express what was in her heart. "After him I love. More than I love life! More than shall I ever love wife!"

Maria turned the implications of Viola's words over in her mind.

"Ay me detested! Ay me beguiled!" protested Olivia.

"And how this male-bonding has gone simply wild," mused Maria.

"Who does beguile you?" asked Viola. "Who does you wrong?"

"Hast thou forgotten?" questioned Olivia. "Is it so long?"

"Come away!" said Orsino, pulling on Viola.

"Wither, my lord?" asked Olivia. Then finally:

"Cesario! Husband! Stay!"

Olivia's cry stunned Orsino. "Husband?" he asked the countess.

"Ay, husband! Can he that deny?"

Viola shook her head. "No, my lord. Not I."

Twelve Nights with Viola & Olivia

Olivia walked up to the two. "Alas, Cesario. It is the baseness of thy fear that makes thee deny thyself."

Olivia motioned to Maria. "My lord, my maid will tell what hath passed between us."

Maria recited: "A contract of eternal love, confirmed by the joinder of your hands. Attested by the holy close of lips, strengthened by the exchanging of rings. And all the ceremony of this compact nay but two hours."

"How can this be?" Viola despaired.

Orsino turned to his most-loved gentleman. "O thou dissembling cub! What wilt thou be when time hath sowed a grizzle on thy case?" Pointing to Olivia, he told Viola, "Farewell and take her:"

Then Orsino warned darkly: "But direct thy feet where thou and I may never meet!"

Without a thought to Orsino's fatal implications, Olivia celebrated her triumph, and pulled Viola away. "My lord, I do protest—" pleaded Viola to Orsino, helplessly.

Checking his rage, Orsino proceeded to lead his men home. "Bring up the horses!"

Suddenly, *Cavaliere* Andreano ran up to the party panicking, while he bled from a cut on his head. "For the love of God, a surgeon! Send one presently to *Cavaliere* Tobi!"

Olivia, who was always shocked by blood, asked: "What's the matter?"

"He has broken my head across and given Tobi a bloody coxcomb too!" said Andreano, "For the love of God, your help!"

"Long Live the Countess!"

Olivia calmly told her gentlewoman, "Maria, tend to the knight."

Maria looked to Andreano; he had only sustained a scratch. "Who would have known the old man had so much blood in him?" she mused.

"Who has done this?" Olivia asked the knight.

"The *Conte's* gentleman, one Cesario," Andreano declared. "We took him for a coward, but he's the very devil!"

Orsino could not believe his ears. "My gentleman Cesario?"

Andreano was stunned to see Viola. "There he is!" Andreano pointed at the count's gentleman. "I'll bring suit for battery against you! Yes, I struck you first, but it's no matter."

Viola was reaching her limit of abuse. "Why do you speak to me? You drew on me! But I hurt you not!"

Sebastiano came running up to Olivia, stopping next to Viola.

"I am sorry, madam, I have hurt your kinsman," he said. "But had it been the brother of my blood, I must have done no less."

Olivia looked at Sebastiano, then at Viola, then back at Sebastiano, and then she realized that the man she had married was not the man she was in love with: The shock stunned her silent.

"You throw a strange regard upon me, and by that I do perceive it hath offended you," he said, as Olivia stood still as a statue.

Twelve Nights with Viola & Olivia

Sebastiano took Olivia's hands and knelt before her. "Pardon me, sweet one, even for the vows we made each other but so late ago," he pleaded.

Olivia directed his attention toward Viola.

"Do I stand there?" he asked. "I never had a brother. I had a sister, whom the waves devoured." He addressed the strange figure.

"What kin are you to me? What countryman? What parentage?"

"Of Messaline," Viola answered. "Sebastos was my father, and Sebastos was my brother, before he went to his watery tomb. If as a spirit, you come to fright us."

Sebastiano smiled at this happy surprise reunion. "A spirit I am indeed; but am in that dimension which from the womb I did participate."

Sebastiano placed his hands on Viola's shoulders. "Were you a woman, I should let my tear fall upon your cheek, and say, 'Thrice-Welcome, drown-ed Viola!'"

"Sebastos, my brother!" exclaimed Viola.

The two embraced, as two siblings that had thought they has lost the other forever.

While they embraced, Olivia asked Maria, "Is it possible?" Maria shook her head. "Nay!" she scoffed. "Were this played upon a stage now, I would condemn it as an improbable fiction!" she scoffed.

Viola and Sebastiano separated. "So comes it lady, you have been mistook," said Sebastiano. "But nature to her bias drew in that."

"Long Live the Countess!"

Orsino, his anger replaced by joy at learning the secret of his gentleman, stepped up to Viola. "Be not amazed; right noble is his blood," he declared. "If this be so, I shall have share of this happy wreck."

"Boy: Thou hast said to me a thousand times," said Orsino to Viola, "Thou shouldst never love woman like to me."

Viola reaffirmed to Orsino: "And all those sayings will I overswear; and all those swearings keep as true in my soul."

"Your master quits you," said Orsino. "And since you called me master for so long, you shall be your master's mistress."

Orsino kissed Viola's delicate hand. Moved by the moment, Orsino's men and Olivia's people applauded the union of these two souls.

They were still congratulating Orsino when two of his officers passed by Olivia's house, leading a man in irons through the town.

"Lord Orsino, noble sir," said the officer. "This is Antonio, the wretched pirate!"

Orsino's face lost all its previous joy. "That face I do remember well; Yet when last I saw it, it was besmeared with the smoke of war."

Sebastiano ran up and embraced his friend. "Antonio! My dear Antonio! How the hours have racked me, since I lost thee!"

Sebastiano held one arm around Antonio as he spoke to Olivia. "This is the Antonio to whom owe I my life. This is he thou vowed to save."

Twelve Nights with Viola & Olivia

Olivia turned to Orsino, curtsied to show homage. "Most noble *Conte*. As our houses shall be united, perchance thou not detain a brother of thy brother."

Orsino thought for a moment, looked at Viola, then Sebastiano, then Antonio, and then nodded in agreement. "This mirth in me persuades a trust that thou art right," said he to Olivia.

"Release this man," he commanded.

Orsino embraced Antonio and kissed him as a family member. "As the brother of my brother, let thee be my new brother too."

As the two men hugged as brothers, all those present applauded their reconciliation.

* * *

As the sun started to set, Olivia ordered that their wedding fete be held in her garden. Musicians were fetched, refreshments were brought out, hasty invitations were made to the leading citizens of the area, and torches were lit; this was not a night to count the cost of lighting oil.

Olivia was sitting with Maria, when she beckoned Adriano.

"Bring her to us, prithee," said Olivia.

"Ay, my lady."

"But first, tell Antonio he is welcome to the house; A fortnight, or as my husband wills."

"At once, my lady." Adriano left the couple. Olivia took some coins from her purse.

"She baffled us both, Maria. Ten ducats are due thee."

"Long Live the Countess!"

"O keep them, my lady:" said Maria, declining the money. She placed her hands over Olivia's, saying: "For a wedding gift."

Viola, still in her gentleman's clothes, curtsied to Olivia.

"Most excellent accomplished lady, the heavens rain odours on you!" said Viola, before giggling in her more accustomed way.

"The knave be an excellent fool," Olivia said to Maria. "Peace, you rogue," humoured the countess.

"My lady hath matter for thee," Maria said to Viola.

"At your service, fair princess!" Viola curtsied to Olivia with an enthusiastic flourish, so glad was she to be a girl again.

"Viola, thou art a sister of me. A sister!" exclaimed the countess. "You are she!"

Viola hid her disquiet. "So shall I be."

"Lady Viola," said Olivia, using the title soon-to-be given to her future sister-in-law, "I vow to thee: Thou shalt be the best *Contessa*, there ever shall be."

Maria stood with her goblet and proclaimed: "All Hail, *Contessa* Viola!"

Olivia raised her own goblet: "Long Live the *Contessa!*" Hearing Olivia's proclamation, her people echoed: "Long Live the *Contessa!*"

Then at a motion from Orsino, his men drew their swords and saluted the new mistress of their house with booming masculine cheers. "Long Live the *Contessa!*"

Twelve Nights with Viola & Olivia

"Long Live the *Contessa*!" cheered everyone, leaving Viola overwhelmed by all the good wishes for her.

And thus, twelve nights from being rescued from the sea, without a penny in her hand, *Nobildonna* Viola was created a *Contessa* of the County of Piscari, in the Duchy of Abruzzi, in the Kingdom of Sicily, within the Empire of Spain, in the reign of Ferdinand II of Aragon, by the grace of God and His Holiness, Pope Leo X. *In Sæcula Sæculorum*. Amen.

THE NEXT BOOK IN
THE NEW COUNTESS SERIES:

"If I Should Tell My History"

By Lady Vanessa S.-G.

Nothing will stop newly-married Countess Olivia from reuniting her new husband and sister-in-law with their mother and uncle — no matter what the leaders of the Church say about it. Meanwhile, she ponders whether to annul the she marriage entered into by accident, while recognizing that her husband is more interested in another man, than she realized at first.

Made in the USA
Middletown, DE
29 May 2023